Jean-Baptiste Cléry

A JOURNAL OF THE TERROR

Being an account of
the occurrences in the Temple
during the confinement of Louis XVI, by
M. Cléry the King's valet-de-chambre,
together with a description of
the last hours of the King,
by the Abbé de Firmont

EDITED BY
SIDNEY
SCOTT

FOLIO PRESS: J. M. DENT
LONDON 1974

Distributed for the Folio Press
202 Great Suffolk Street, London SE1 by
J. M. DENT & SONS LTD
Aldine House, Albemarle Street, London W1

Folio Society first edition of 1955,
printed by letterpress, with collotype illustrations,
reprinted by photolitho in 1974

ISBN: 0 460 04154 1

PRINTED IN GREAT BRITAIN
at the University Printing House, Cambridge
Set in Fournier type
Bound by J. M. Dent & Sons Ltd, Letchworth

CONTENTS

INTRODUCTION

THE two memoirs of which this book consists are those of Cléry, valet-de-chambre to Louis XVI during his imprisonment in the Temple, and of the Abbé Edgeworth de Firmont, who attended the King during his last hours.

To set the scene, it may be as well to go back a little in time, and recall the various steps which had been taken along the path of revolution before the imprisonment of the Royal Family.

The French Revolution was not one great uprising on the part of what nowadays would be called the underprivileged against their rich and powerful oppressors. Rather was it four separate revolutions, one after another, each with a different aim, and each carried out by different leaders. First came the Orléanist revolution, of 1789, which was in effect 'the beginning of the end' of the ancient régime. This was followed in rapid succession by the Girondist revolution of 1792, the Jacobin revolution of the following year, and, finally, by the Thermidorian revolution of 1794.

In May 1789 the States-General met, in order to deal with the financial situation of the country, which had got beyond the control of the King and his Ministers. The Third Estate insisted that the States-General sit as one chamber, the 'National Assembly', and the King, ready as always to make concessions, ordered the other two Estates, the *noblesse* and the clergy, to join them. Paris seethed with excitement—which culminated in the attack on the Bastille in July—and formed a municipal government, the Commune. In the country, many of the peasantry rose against their seigneurs. The following month, a Constitution was planned on the basis of the doctrine of the Rights of Man.

On 5 October 1789 a mob from Paris marched on Versailles and, the next day, brought the King to the Tuileries, a virtual prisoner. Louis became increasingly dissatisfied with his position: he was in conflict with the Assembly, and his authority and prestige were constantly weakened. In June 1791 he made the fatal mistake of attempting to leave the country, but he and the Royal Family were arrested at Varennes, and brought back to Paris. The French people in general regarded this attempt as an appeal for foreign intervention, and many extremists openly called for the establishment of a republic. In fact, however, the King was only suspended from his functions until three months later when he took the oath to uphold the new constitution.

In April 1792 France declared war on Austria, and the following month Austria's ally Prussia joined in the war against France. In July the Prussian commander, the Duke of Brunswick, issued a manifesto threatening Paris with dire penalties if any harm were done to the French Royal Family. This strengthened the French people's suspicions that Louis was a traitor, playing into the hands of his country's enemies.

The Paris Commune then took control of the situation; the dethronement of the King was mooted in the Assembly, and Louis was persuaded to leave the

Tuileries early on the morning of 10 August and seek the shelter of the Assembly, on the grounds that it was impossible to count on the loyalty of the National Guard. The King and his family were received with apparent courtesy by the deputies, and were given places in the reporters' box, where they heard the debate suspending Louis from his functions.

Meanwhile, soon after the King left, the rabble attacked the Tuileries and the Swiss guard defending it fired on the crowd. When the King heard of the fighting, he sent a message to the Swiss to lay down their arms and retire. He had been hoping to avoid bloodshed, but most of the Swiss were subsequently massacred by the mob. 'I went this morning', wrote the Englishman, Dr John Moore, who was in Paris at the time, 'to see the places where the action of yesterday happened. The naked bodies of the Swiss . . . lay exposed on the ground. . . . Of about 800 or 1000 of these . . . I am told there are not 200 left alive.'

The same day the King was suspended from his functions, and the newly formed Commune decided that it was necessary to find some secure place of imprisonment for the Royal Family. The first choice, the Luxembourg, being too difficult to defend against possible rescue, they finally decided upon the tower of the Temple.

The Temple took its name from the Order of Knights Templar, which had acquired immense wealth on account of the fact that it was exempt from all taxation, and in its heyday owned at least a quarter of the city of Paris. Originally the headquarters of the Order, the buildings survived as a fortress, a prison, and a town residence for the Grand Prior of the Temple, a sinecure office. At the time of the outbreak of the Revolution, the property within the walls consisted of three different sets of buildings: first, the palace of the Comte d'Artois, afterwards to ascend the throne as King Charles X; secondly, the former *Commanderie* of the Knights—chapter-house, cloisters, church, etc.; and lastly, a vast group of private houses which formed a small town within the walls, and had in 1789 a population of some 4000 persons.

The great tower, which was chosen by the Commune to be the prison of the Royal Family, was in such a state of disrepair that Louis XVI and his family were provisionally lodged in the little tower adjoining, which was hurriedly furnished with furniture brought from the palace. The King was moved to the great tower on 30 September, and the Queen, her children, and the King's sister, Madame Elizabeth, joined him there on 26 October. The tower was razed to the ground in 1808, and the land sold. The palace was also sold, and became first a convent and then a barracks, and was finally demolished in 1853.

Jean-Baptiste Cant Hanet Cléry, the author of the following memoirs was born at Jardy, near Versailles, on 11 May 1759. Cléry's family had been in the service of the French Royal Family since the time of Louis XIV, and Cléry, as a child, used to meet his future master Louis XVI in the park of Versailles. Cléry and his brother Hanet went into the service of the Princesse de Guéménée, who became governess to the royal children. In 1785 he became *valet de chambre* to the newly-born Duke of Normandy, later Dauphin. Cléry was with the Royal Family on 5–6 October 1789 when they were brought by the mob from Versailles to Paris, and again in the Tuileries on 9–10 August 1792, when the palace was attacked. When he heard of the imprisonment in the Temple prison, Cléry asked Pétion, Mayor of Paris, to be allowed to wait on the Royal Family in their prison. Eventually Cléry alone of the royal servants was left to attend to the Royal Family, and neither the threats nor the bad treatment he received from the municipal officers in charge of the prison, diminished his devotion. Louis XVI, in his will, paid homage to Cléry's devotion and recommended him to his son.

Henry Essex Edgeworth de Firmont, author of the second Memoir, was the son of Robert Edgeworth, rector of Edgeworthstown in Ireland, and was born in 1745. When he was only three years old his father became a Roman Catholic, resigned his living, and went to live in Toulouse, where the boy was educated in the Jesuit College. In 1769, after his father's death, Henry went to live in Paris, in order to be trained for the priesthood, with the intention of becoming a missionary. On taking Holy Orders, however, he decided to stay in Paris in order that he might devote himself especially to the English-speaking Roman Catholics in the city. After the outbreak of the Revolution he became confessor to Madame Elizabeth, by whom he was recommended to the King during his captivity in the Temple.

The text of Cléry's Journal on which this book is based is that of the first English edition, published simultaneously with the French in London in 1798. Thinking it best to retain the flavour of the original I have made few changes to the translation, except where it differed considerably from the French. I have also endeavoured to translate de Firmont in a style comparable with that of the original French.

W. S. S.

SELBORNE

ACKNOWLEDGEMENTS

The Editor and Publishers wish to acknowledge their indebtedness for kind assistance received in the preparation of this book from Miss E. J. Cruickshanks, Sir John Elliot, M. Jacques Guignard of the Bibliothèque Nationale, Mlle Levent of the Musée Carnavalet, and le Comte Jean de la Monnereye, erstwhile Director of the Bibliothèque Historique de la Ville de Paris.

CLÉRY'S JOURNAL

OF

OCCURRENCES AT THE TEMPLE
DURING THE CONFINEMENT
OF LOUIS XVI, KING OF FRANCE

I WAS in the service of the King of France and his august Family five months in the Tower of the Temple, and notwithstanding the vigilance of the Municipal Officers who were the keepers of it, I found means, by one way or other, to make memorandums of the principal occurrences that took place within that prison.

Although I have been since induced to arrange those memorandums in the form of a Journal, my design is rather to furnish materials to such as shall hereafter write the History of the melancholy end of the unfortunate Louis XVI, than to compose Memoirs myself, which is above my talents and pretensions.

Having been the only continual witness of the insults which the King and his Family were made to suffer, I alone can report and attest them with exactness; I shall accordingly confine myself to publishing a detail of the facts simply, impartially, and without mixing my own opinions.

Although I had been an attendant on the Royal Family from the year 1782, and from the nature of my situation have been witness to the most disastrous events in the course of the Revolution, it would be deviating from my subject to describe them; indeed, most of them are already to be found in various works. I shall therefore begin this Journal at the crisis of the tenth of August, 1792: that dreadful day, on which a small number of men overturned a Throne that had been established fourteen centuries, threw their King into fetters, and precipitated France into an abyss of calamity.

O N the tenth of August I was in waiting on the Dauphin. From the morning of the ninth the agitation of the public mind was extreme: crowds assembled everywhere throughout Paris, and the plan of the conspirators was known beyond a doubt at the Tuileries. The tocsin was to be rung at midnight in every part of the town, and the Marseillais,* on being joined by the inhabitants of the faubourg St Antoine, were to march immediately and besiege the Palace. Confined by the nature of my employment to the apartments of the young Prince, in attendance on his person, I knew but partially what passed out of doors, and I shall give an account of those events only to which I was witness that day, when so many different scenes were exhibited, even in the Palace.

In the evening of the ninth at half past eight o'clock, after having attended the Dauphin to his bed, I went from the Tuileries with the view of learning the sentiments of the public. The courts of the Palace were filled with about eight thousand National Guards,† of different Sections, who were disposed to defend the

---

* Barbaroux had written from Paris to the Jacobin mayor of Marseilles, Mouraille, asking him to send '600 men who would know how to die'. On 30 July, 516 Federals, or members of the New National Guard, excellent middle-class citizens from Toulon and Marseilles, came into Paris after crossing France at 18 miles a day dragging their cannons all the way. They brought Rouget de Lisle's new song with them.

† A citizen army established in August 1789, after the grave disorders of July, to maintain order in Paris. It was organized by Lafayette its first commander. Its strength in Paris was over 30,000 men, and its officers were elected.

King. I made my way to the Palais-Royal, where I found almost all the avenues closed: some of the National Guards were there under arms, ready to march to the Tuileries in order to support the battalions that had gone before them; but a mob, set in motion by revolutionary leaders, filled the adjacent streets, and rent the air on all sides with their clamours.

I returned about eleven o'clock to the Palace by the King's apartments. The attendants of the Court, and those in waiting on His Majesty, were collecting together, and under great anxiety. I passed on to the Dauphin's room, which I had scarcely entered when I heard the tocsin ringing and the drums beating to arms in every quarter of the town. I remained in the great hall till five in the morning, in company with Madame de St Brice, woman of the bedchamber to the young Prince. At six, the King came down into the courts of the Palace, and reviewed the National Guards and the Swiss,* who swore to defend him. The Queen and her children followed the King; and although some seditious voices were heard among the ranks, they were soon drowned in the repeated cries of *Vive le Roi! Vive la Nation!*

The Tuileries not appearing to be in immediate danger of attack, I again went out, and walked along

---

* The Swiss Guards, a regiment of Household troops which totalled 2,248 men in 1789, were mercenaries recruited in the French and German cantons of Switzerland. The Legislative Assembly had ordered the King to disband them, but he did not do so. On the contrary, on 9 August the Swiss Guards quartered at Reuil and Courbevoie, near Paris, had been summoned to the Tuileries as reinforcements.

the quays as far as the Pont-Neuf, everywhere meeting
bands of armed men, whose evil intentions were very
evident; some had pikes, others had pitch-forks,
hatchets or iron bars. The battalion of the Marseillais
were marching in the greatest order, with their cannon
and lighted matches, inviting the people to follow
them, and 'assist', as they said, 'in dislodging the
tyrant, and proclaiming his deposition to the National
Assembly'. I was but too well convinced of what was
approaching, yet impelled by a sense of duty, I
hastened before this battalion, and made immediately
for the Tuileries, where I saw a large body of National
Guards, pouring out in disorder through the garden
gate opposite to the Pont-Royal. Sorrow was visible
on the countenances of most of them, and several
were heard to say: 'We swore this morning to defend
the King, and in the moment of his greatest danger we
are deserting him.' Others, in the interest of the conspirators, were abusing and threatening their fellow-
soldiers, whom they forced away. Thus did the well-
disposed suffer themselves to be overawed by the
seditious, and that culpable weakness, which had all
along been productive of the evils of the Revolution,
gave birth to the calamities of this day.

After many attempts to gain admission into the
Palace, a porter at one of the gates recognized me and
suffered me to pass. I ran immediately to the King's
apartments, and begged one of his attendants to inform
His Majesty of all I had seen and heard.

At seven o'clock the distress was increased by the
cowardice of several battalions that successively

deserted the Tuileries. About four or five hundred of the National Guards remained at their post, and displayed equal fidelity and courage: they were placed indiscriminately with the Swiss Guards within the Palace, at the different staircases, and at all the entrances. These troops having spent the night without taking any refreshment, I eagerly engaged with others of the King's servants in providing them with bread and wine, and encouraging them not to desert the Royal Family. It was at this time that the King gave the command, within the Palace, to the Maréchal de Mailly, the Duc du Châtelet, the Comte de Puységur, the Baron de Vioménil, the Comte d'Hervilly, the Marquis du Pujet, and other faithful officers. The persons of the Court and the servants were distributed in the different halls, having first sworn to defend the King to the last drop of their blood. We were about three or four hundred strong, but our only arms were swords or pistols.

At eight o'clock the danger became more imminent. The Legislative Assembly was convened at the Riding-School, facing the garden of the Tuileries; the King had sent several messages to them, communicating the situation in which he then was, at the same time inviting them to appoint a deputation to assist him with their counsel; but the Assembly, though the Palace was threatened with an attack before their eyes, returned no answer.

Some few minutes after, the Department of Paris, and several Municipal Officers made their appearance, with Rœderer, then Procurator-General-Syndic,* at

* Procureur-General-Syndic was the title of the law officer of the Directory of the Department of Paris.

their head. Rœderer, doubtless in concert with the conspirators, strongly persuaded the King to go with his Family to the Assembly, asserting that he could no longer depend upon the National Guard, and declaring that if he remained in the Palace, neither the Department nor the Municipality of Paris would any longer answer for his safety. The King heard him without emotion, and then retired to his chamber with the Queen, the Ministers, and a few attendants, whence he soon returned to go with his Family to the Assembly. He was attended by a detachment of Swiss and National Guards. None of the attendants, except the Princesse de Lamballe and the Marquise de Tourzel, who was governess of the Children of France,* were permitted to follow the Royal Family. The Marquise de Tourzel, that she might not be separated from the young Prince, was obliged to leave her daughter, then seventeen years of age, at the Tuileries, in the midst of the soldiers. It was now near nine o'clock.

Compelled to remain in the apartments, I awaited with terror the consequences of the step the King had taken, and went to a window that looked upon the garden. In about half an hour after the Royal Family had gone to the Assembly, I saw four heads carried on pikes along the terrace of the Feuillants,† towards the building where the Legislative Body was sitting. This was, I believe, the signal for attacking the Palace, for

* *Les Enfants de France* was the ceremonial term used to describe the children of the Sovereign.

† The most moderate of the revolutionary clubs, founded by the Constitutionalist party.

at the same instant there began a dreadful firing of cannon and musketry. The Palace was everywhere pierced with balls and bullets. As the King was gone, every man endeavoured to take care of himself, but all the exits were blocked, and certain death seemed to await us. I ran from place to place, and finding the apartments and staircases already strewn with dead bodies, took the resolution of leaping from one of the windows in the Queen's room down upon the terrace, whence I made across the parterre with the utmost speed to reach the Pont-Tournant. A body of Swiss, who had gone before me, were rallying under the trees. Finding myself between two fires, I ran back in order to gain the new flight of steps leading up to the terrace on the water-side, intending to throw myself over the wall upon the quay, but was prevented by the constant fire that was kept up on the Pont-Royal. I continued my way on the same side till I came to the gate of the Dauphin's garden, where some Marseillais, who had just butchered several of the Swiss, were stripping them. One of them came up to me with a bloody sword in his hand, saying: 'How, citizen! without arms? take this sword, and help us to kill.' However, another Marseillais seized it. I was, as he observed, without arms, and fortunately in a plain frock[-coat]; for if anything had betrayed my situation in the Palace, I should not have escaped.

Some of the Swiss, who were pursued, took refuge in an adjoining stable; I concealed myself in the same place. They were soon cut to pieces close to me. On hearing the cries of these wretched victims, M. le Dreux, the master of the house, ran up, and I seized that opportunity of going in, when, without knowing me, M. le Dreux and his wife invited me to stay till the danger was over. In my pocket were letters and newspapers directed to the Prince Royal, and a card of admission to the Tuileries, on which my name and the nature of my employment were written; papers that could not have failed to betray me, and which I had just time to throw away before a body of armed men came into the house, to see if any of the Swiss were concealed in it. I pretended, by the advice of M. le Dreux, to be working at some drawings that were lying on a large table. After a fruitless search, these fellows, their hands dyed with blood, stopped and coolly related the murders of which they had been guilty. I remained in this asylum from ten o'clock in the morning till four in the afternoon, having before my eyes the sight of the horrors that were committed in the Place Louis Quinze. Of the men, some were continuing the slaughter, and others cutting off the heads of those who were already slain; while the women, lost to all sense of shame, were committing the most indecent mutilations on the dead bodies, from which they tore pieces of flesh, and carried them in triumph.

In the course of the day, Madame de Rambaut, one of the women of the bedchamber to the Dauphin, having escaped with great difficulty from the massacre at the Tuileries, came for refuge to the house where I was; but we made signs to each other not to speak. The sons of our hosts, who soon after came in from the National Assembly, informed us that the authority of the King had been suspended, and that he was kept in sight, with the Royal Family, in the shorthand writer's box,* so that it was impossible to approach his person.

On hearing this I would fain have gone home to my wife and children at a country house about five leagues from Paris, where we had lived above two years; but the barriers were shut, and I also thought myself bound not to desert Madame de Rambaut. We agreed therefore to take the road to Versailles, where she resided, and the sons of our host accompanied us. We crossed the Pont Louis Seize, which was covered with the naked carcasses of men already in a state of putrefaction from the great heat of the weather, and, after many risks, escaped from Paris through an unguarded breach in the walls.

In the plain of Grenelle we were met by peasants on horseback, who, threatening us with their arms, called to us from a distance, to stop or that we should have our brains blown out. One of them, taking me for one of the King's Guards, levelled his piece at me, and was going to fire, when another proposed to take us to the Municipality of Vaugirard, saying: 'There's a score of them already, the harvest will be the greater.' At the Municipality our hosts were known, but the Mayor, addressing himself to me, asked why I was not

* In the original *la loge du rédacteur du Logographe*, a box set apart for the shorthand writers of a paper called the *Logographe*, which professed to give the debates word for word. (*Note to original English edition.*)

at my post when the country was in danger? 'Why', said he, 'do you quit Paris? It has the appearance of bad designs.' 'Ay, ay,' cried the mob, 'to prison; away to prison with the aristocrats.' I replied that it was for the very purpose of going to my post that I was on the road to Versailles, where I resided, and where my post was, as theirs was at Vaugirard. Madame de Rambaut was also interrogated, and our hosts having declared that we spoke the truth, we were furnished with passports. I have reason to bless GOD that I was not taken to their prison, for they had just before sent thither two and twenty of the King's Guards, who were afterwards removed to the Abbaye [Prison], where they were massacred on the second of September following.

From Vaugirard to Versailles we were continually stopped by patrols to have our passports examined. Having conducted Madame de Rambaut to her relations, I delayed not a moment to repair to my own family; but the fall I had received in leaping from the window at the Tuileries, the fatigue of walking twelve leagues, and the painful reflections of my mind upon the deplorable events that had just taken place, were too much for me to bear, and threw me into a very high fever. For three days I kept my bed, but my impatience to know the fate of the King overcame my disorder, and I returned to Paris.

On my arrival on the evening of the thirteenth, I learnt that the Royal Family were just sent to the Temple after having been detained at the Feuillants since the tenth; that the King had chosen M. de

Chamilly, his first valet de chambre, to wait upon him; and that M. Huë, usher of the King's chamber, and for whom the place of the Dauphin's first valet de chambre had been intended, was to wait upon the young Prince.

[The Memoirs of M. Huë give the following account of the arrival at the Temple:

'With hearts filled with sadness and foreboding, the Royal Family arrived at the Temple. Santerre* was the first person they met in the courtyard. He made the Municipal Officers a sign which at the moment I could not understand, but I have since realised that it was to instruct them to conduct the King immediately into the Tower. A shake of the head on the part of the officers announced that it was not yet time.

'The Royal Family first entered the part of the buildings known as the palace, from the fact that it was the customary residence of the Comte d'Artois whenever he came to Paris. The Officers kept close to the King, wearing their hats, and giving him no other title than that of Monsieur. A man with a long beard, whom I had first of all taken for a Jew, repeated this word on every possible occasion. Some of the Officers who behaved so badly, not to say cruelly, at this time, later appeared to repent their conduct and to be sincerely sorry for the King's imprisonment.

---

* This unspeakable ruffian, by profession a brewer, was the leader of the Faubourg St Antoine Section, the most revolutionary part of Paris. As commander of a battalion of the National Guard, he played a vital part in the events of 10 August. He became commander-in-chief of the National Guard in 1793.

'The day when the Royal Family were shut up in the Temple seemed to be a feast day for the Parisians; crowds gathered round the buildings, shouting out *Vive la Nation!* Lanterns, placed on the projections of the outside walls, lit up this scene of barbarity.

'In the belief that it was the *palace* which had been chosen to be his lodging, the King wished to see the apartments. While the Officers took a cruel pleasure in letting him continue in this error, the better to enjoy his later discomfiture, His Majesty was pleased to distribute various lodgings. Soon the interior of the Temple was filled with numerous officials. The orders were so strict that one could not take a step without being stopped. In the midst of this crowd the King showed the calm that comes of a good conscience.

'At ten o'clock supper was served. During the meal, a short one, Manuel* stood beside the King. As soon as it was over, the Royal Family entered the salon. From this moment Louis XVI was abandoned to this

* Louis Pierre Manuel, although not one of the best known of the revolutionaries, was in many respects one of the most revolting characters among their ranks and was one of the moving spirits behind the terrible September massacres. It can be said of him that he was responsible for removing imprisonment for debt from poor debtors; it was also to him that Madame de Tourzel, Madame de Staël and Beaumarchais owed their freedom, and he did his utmost to save the Princesse de Lamballe, without success; but it is more than probable that he was heavily bribed in each case. All that can be said for him is that he was greatly impressed by the behaviour of the King and the Royal Family in the Temple, and spoke in their favour on several occasions. This eventually resulted in his being arrested under the Law of Suspects, tried, and guillotined.

factious "commune" which surrounded him with guardians, or rather gaolers, known as Commissioners. When they entered the Temple, the Municipal Officers had warned the servants that the Royal Family were not going to sleep in the palace, but were only going to occupy it in the day-time: we were not surprised, therefore, to hear one of the Commissioners, about eleven o'clock, order us to take the little linen and clothing that it had been possible to get, and follow him.

'One of the Officers preceded me, carrying a lantern, by whose feeble light I tried to discover the place destined for the Royal Family. We stopped in front of a building which the darkness made me think very large. Without being able to distinguish anything clearly, I saw nevertheless a difference between the design of this building and that of the palace we had just left. The front part of the roof which appeared to me to be surmounted with pinnacles which I took for steeples, was edged with battlements, with lanterns every here and there.

'In spite of the light these shed, I could not make out what this building, built on an extraordinary plan, or at least one quite new to me, could possibly be.

'One of the Officers, breaking the dreary silence which he had kept during our walk, said to me, "Your master has been accustomed to gilded halls. Well, now he is going to see how we lodge the assassins of the people! Follow me."

'I went up several steps: a narrow, low doorway led me to a spiral staircase. When I left this principal staircase for a still smaller one which led me to the second floor, I found that I was in a tower. I entered a room lit by one single window, largely destitute of even the most necessary furniture, and having only one poor bed and three or four seats. "That's where your master will sleep", the Officer said to me. Chamilly had now rejoined me, and we looked at each other without saying a word. The Officer threw us, as if it were a favour, a pair of sheets, and left us for a few moments alone.

'An alcove, with neither hangings nor curtains, contained a small bed with an old bug-ridden mattress. We worked hard to get both the room and the bed as clean as possible. The King came in; he showed neither surprise nor anger. The walls of the room were hung with pictures, for the most part barely decent: he took them down himself, saying "I do not wish my daughter to see such things." His Majesty went to bed and slept peacefully; Chamilly and I stayed all night seated by his bedside, respectfully admiring the calm of this irreproachable man, fighting against misfortune and conquering it by courage. "He who can exercise such control over himself", we said, "is he not made to command others!" The sentries placed at the door of the room were relieved every hour, and each day the Municipal Officers were changed.']

The Princesse de Lamballe, the Marquise de Tourzel, and Mademoiselle Pauline de Tourzel had accompanied the Queen; and Madame Thibaut, Madame Bazire, Madame Navarre, and Madame St Brice, four of the women of the bedchamber, attended Her Majesty, the Prince and Princesses.

I now lost all hope of continuing with the Dauphin, and was going to return into the country, when, on the sixteenth day of the King's confinement, I was informed that every person who was in the Tower with the Royal Family had been taken up in the night; that after being examined before the Council of the Commune of Paris, they had been all sent to the prison de la Force, except M. Huë, who was carried back to the Temple to attend upon the King; and that Pétion,* then Mayor, was commissioned to point out two persons more. Upon this intelligence I determined to try every means to recover my place about the Prince, and went to Pétion, who said that as I belonged to the King's household I should not be able to obtain the consent of the Council General of the Commune; but on my citing the instance of M. Huë, who had just been sent by the same council to attend upon the King, he

* Jérome Pétion de Villeneuve, a lawyer from Chartres, was elected a Deputy to the States-General in 1789. He was a man devoid of even the most ordinary ability, but so inordinately vain that he believed he had been especially chosen to regenerate mankind. He at once threw himself into the party of the extremists, and was one of the three men sent to bring back the King after his arrest at Varennes. He was elected Mayor of Paris in 1791. At the King's trial he voted for the death penalty. Accused of responsibility for the September massacres, he was proscribed with the Girondins, and fled first to Calvados, and then to the Gironde, but could find no safe asylum anywhere. Being without hope, he committed suicide, and his body was afterwards found lying in a cornfield, partially devoured by wolves.

promised to support a memorial which I put into his hands. However, I observed to him that it would be first necessary to inform the King of the step I had taken, and two days afterwards he wrote to His Majesty in the following terms:

SIRE,

The valet de chambre who has attended the Prince Royal from his infancy wishes to be continued in his service, and as I think it will be agreeable to you, I have granted his request, &c.

His Majesty wrote in answer, that he accepted my service for his Son, and I was accordingly conducted to the Temple. I was searched, informed of the manner in which it was expected that I should behave, and the same day, the twenty-sixth of August, at eight o'clock in the evening, entered the Tower.

I T would be difficult for me to describe the impression made upon me by the sight of this august and unfortunate Family. The Queen first spoke to me, and after some expressions full of goodness, she added, 'You will attend my son, and concert with M. Huë as to us.' I was so overcome that I could scarcely make an answer.

At supper, the Queen and the Princesses, who for eight days had been deprived of their female attendants, asked me if I could comb their hair. I replied that I would do anything they desired, and a Municipal

Louis XVI   Marie-Antoinette

The Dauphin

Madame Elizabeth   Madame Royale

Officer came up to me, and told me, loud enough to be heard by all, to be more circumspect in my replies. A beginning that alarmed me.*

For the first eight days of my being at the Temple I had no communication out-of-doors, M. Huë being the only person commissioned to ask for and receive whatever was necessary for the Royal Family, on whom we attended jointly and without distinction. With respect to the King himself, I had only to dress him in the morning and roll his hair at night. Perceiving that I was incessantly watched by the Municipal Officers, who took umbrage at the slightest trifle, I very cautiously avoided any indiscretion, which would infallibly have been my ruin.

On the second of September, there were great tumults about the Temple. The King and the Family having come down as usual to walk in the garden, a Municipal Officer that followed the King said to one of his associates, 'We were wrong in allowing them to

* An idea of the precautions taken by these Municipal Officers is given by Turgy in his *Fragments historiques sur le Temple.* 'As soon as the King arrived at the Temple, the most stringent precautions were ordered. This is the way in which my service had to be carried on. Before dinner, or indeed before any meal, I had to go to the Council Chamber and ask for two of the officers to come, who themselves laid the dishes, and tasted the food to make sure there was nothing hidden in it. I could only fill the decanters and make the coffee in their presence.... They accompanied me to the dining-room, and only allowed me to lay the table when they had examined it above and below: I had to unfold the cloth and the napkins in front of them: they cut each roll of bread in half, and searched the inside with a fork, or even with their fingers.'

walk this afternoon.' I had taken notice in the morning
that the Commissioners from the Municipality were
uneasy. They made the Royal Family return in a
violent hurry, but they were scarcely assembled in the
Queen's chamber, when two of the Officers, who were
not on duty at the Tower, came in, and one of them,
whose name was Mathieu, formerly a Capuchin, thus
addressed the King: 'You are unacquainted, Sir, with
what is passing. The Country is in the greatest danger,
the enemy have entered Champagne, and the King of
Prussia is marching to Chalons.* You will have to
answer for all the mischief that may follow. We know
that we, our wives and children must perish, but the
people shall be avenged. You shall be the first to die;
however, there is yet time and you may—' Here the
King replied that he had done everything for the
people, and had nothing to reproach himself with. On
which the same fellow, turning to M. Huë, said: 'The
Council of the Commune have charged me to take you
into custody.' 'Whom?' cried the King. 'Your valet
de chambre' was the reply. The King desired to know
of what crime he was accused, but not being able to
obtain information, became the more uneasy for his
fate, and recommended him with great concern to the
two Officers. Seals were put, in the presence of M.
Huë, on the small room occupied by him, and he was
taken away at six in the evening, after having been

* In the month of August the Prussians had taken Longwy,
and Verdun fell on 2 September. The French army, under the
command of Dumouriez, was at length able to force them to
retreat after the action at Valmy on 20 September.

twenty days in the Temple.* Mathieu, as he was going out, told me to take care how I conducted myself, 'For', said he, 'it may be your turn next.'

The King then called me to him and gave me some papers, which he had received from M. Huë, containing accounts of expenses. The disturbed looks of the Municipal Officers, and the clamours of the populace in the neighbourhood of the Tower, affected him exceedingly. After the King went to bed, he desired me to sleep near him, and I placed my bed by His Majesty's.

On the third of September, His Majesty, when I was dressing him, asked me if I had heard any news of M. Huë, and if I knew anything of the commotions in Paris. I told him that in the course of the night I had heard an Officer say the people were going to the prisons; but I would try if I could learn anything more. 'Take care', said His Majesty, 'not to expose yourself, for we should then be left alone; and, indeed, I fear it is their intention to put strangers about us.'

At eleven in the forenoon, the King having joined his Family in the Queen's chamber, a Municipal Officer desired me to go up to the King's, where I found Manuel and some members of the Commune. Manuel asked me what the King had said of M. Huë's being taken away. I answered that it had made His Majesty very uneasy. 'He will come to no harm,' said he, 'but I am commanded to inform the King that he is not to return, but that the Council will put a person in his place. You may go and break this to him.' I begged to be excused,

* Though twice arrested, M. Huë escaped with his life.

adding that the King desired to see him respecting several things of which the Royal Family stood in great need. Manuel could scarcely prevail upon himself to go down to the chamber where His Majesty was. He communicated the order of the Council of the Commune, concerning M. Huë, and informed him that another person was to be sent. 'By no means,' replied the King, 'I will make use of my Son's valet de chambre, and if the Council object to that, I will wait upon myself, I am resolved.' His Majesty then mentioned that the Family were in want of linen, and other clothing. Manuel said he would go and make it known to the Council, and retired. I asked him, as I conducted him out, if the tumults continued, and his answers excited my apprehensions that the populace might visit the Temple. 'You have undertaken a perilous service,' added he, 'and I advise you to prepare all your courage.'

At one o'clock the King and the Family expressed a desire to walk, but were refused. When they were dining, drums were heard, and soon after the cries of the populace. The Royal Family rose from table with great uneasiness, and assembled in the Queen's chamber. I went down to dine with Tison and his wife, who were employed for the service of the Tower.

We were scarcely seated when a head on the point of a pike was held to the window. Tison's wife gave a violent scream, which the murderers supposed to have proceeded from the Queen, and we heard the savages laughing immoderately. Imagining that Her Majesty was still at dinner, they placed their victim in such a manner that it could not escape her sight. The head was the Princesse de Lamballe's, which, though bleeding, was not disfigured, and her fine light hair, still curling, waved round the pike.

I ran instantly to the King. My countenance was so altered by terror that it was perceived by the Queen, from whom it was necessary to hide the cause; I wished only to warn the King, or Madame Elizabeth, but the two Commissioners of the Municipality were present. 'Why don't you go and dine?' said the Queen. I replied that I was not well; and at that moment another Municipal Officer, entering the Tower, came and spoke to his associates with an air of mystery. On the King's asking if his Family was in safety, they answered: 'It has been reported that you and your Family are gone from the Tower, and the people are calling for you to appear at the window, but we shall not suffer it, for they ought to show more confidence in their Magistrates.'

In the meantime the clamour without increased, and insults addressed to the Queen were distinctly heard. Another Municipal Officer came in, followed by four men, deputed by the populace to ascertain whether the Royal Family was, or was not, in the Tower. One of them, accoutred in the uniform of the National Guards, with two epaulettes, and a huge sabre in his hand, insisted that the prisoners should show themselves at the windows, but the Municipal Officers would not allow it. This fellow then said to the Queen, in the most indecent manner: 'They want to keep you from seeing de Lamballe's head, which has been brought you that you may know how the people avenge themselves upon their tyrants: I advise you to show yourself, if you would not have them come up here.' At this threat the Queen fainted away; I flew to support her, and Madame Elizabeth assisted me in placing her upon a chair, while her children, melting into tears, endeavoured by their caresses to bring her to herself. The wretch kept looking on, and the King, with a firm voice, said to him: 'We are prepared for everything, Sir, but you might have dispensed with relating this horrible disaster to the Queen.' Their purpose being accomplished, he went away with his companions.

The Queen coming to herself, mingled her tears with those of her children, and all the Family removed to Madame Elizabeth's chamber, where the noises of the mob were less heard. I remained a short time in the Queen's, and looking out at the window, through the blinds, I again saw the Princesse de Lamballe's head. The person that carried it was mounted upon the rubbish of some houses that were ordered to be pulled down for the purpose of isolating the Tower: another stood behind him, holding the heart of that unfortunate Princess, covered with blood, on the point of a sabre. The crowd being inclined to force the gate of the Tower, was harangued by a Municipal Officer, named Daujon, and I very distinctly heard him say: 'The head of Antoinette does not belong to you; the Departments have their respective rights to it; France has confided these great culprits to the care of the City of Paris; and it is your part to assist in securing them, until the national justice takes vengeance for the people.' He was more than an hour debating with them before he could get them away.

On the evening of the same day, one of the Commissioners told me that the mob had attempted to rush in with their four deputies, and to carry into the Tower the body of the Princesse de Lamballe, naked and bloody as it had been dragged from the prison de la Force to the Temple: that some Municipal Officers, after struggling with them, had hung a tri-coloured ribbon across the principal gate as a bar against them; that the Commune of Paris, General Santerre, and the National Assembly had been all called upon in vain for assistance to put a stop to designs which no pains were taken to conceal; and that for six hours it was very doubtful whether the Royal Family would not be massacred. In truth, that faction was not yet sufficiently powerful; the chiefs, although they were unanimous as to the regicide, were not so as to the means of perpetrating it, and the Assembly were perhaps willing that any other hands but theirs should be the instruments of the Conspirators. It struck me as a remarkable circumstance that the Municipal Officer, after the narrative he gave me, made me pay him five-and-forty sous, which the tri-coloured ribbon had cost.

At eight in the evening all was calm in the neighbourhood of the Tower, but the same tranquillity was far from reigning throughout Paris, where the massacres were continued for four or five days.* I had

* These were the terrible 'Massacres of September', in which over a thousand men and women were murdered, after trials

an opportunity when the King was going to bed, to tell him of the commotions I had seen, and the particulars I had heard. He asked me which of the Municipal Officers had shown most firmness in defending the lives of his Family; I mentioned Daujon as having stopped the impetuosity of the people, though nothing was farther from his heart than good will to His Majesty. He did not come to the Tower again for four months, and then the King, recollecting his conduct, thanked him.

T HE day following was still very melancholy from the recollections of the preceding one, but the scenes of horror I have been relating, having been followed with some degree of tranquillity, the Royal Family resumed the uniform mode of life which they

---

which were nothing but mockeries. The Archbishop of Arles and more than a hundred Priests who had refused to take the Oath and were imprisoned in the Convent of the Carmelites, were there done to death; the former Minister of Foreign Affairs, Montmorin, and the Princesse de Lamballe were others of the victims. The chief responsibility for these massacres undoubtedly lies with Marat and Danton, who instigated them. Their proclaimed intention was to put to death all who had been arrested as sympathisers with the enemies of France, before the Germans had an opportunity to carry out their threat of taking 'an exemplary and never to be forgotten vengeance on the city of Paris'. It is more probable, however, that the real purpose in the minds of the bands of murderers was the satisfaction of cruel and bestial instincts. For a full account of these terrible days, see G. Lenôtre, *Les Massacres de Septembre*, 1907.

had adopted on their arrival at the Temple. That the particulars may be the more easily understood, I shall here give a description of the small Tower, in which the King was then confined.

It stood with its back against the great Tower, without any interior communication, and formed a long square, flanked by two turrets. In one of these turrets there was a narrow staircase that led from the first floor to a gallery on the platform: in the other were small rooms answering to each story of the Tower. (See plan p. 57.)

The body of the building was four stories high. The first consisted of an antechamber, a dining-room, and a small room in the turret, where there was a library, containing from twelve to fifteen hundred volumes.

The second story was divided nearly in the same manner. The largest room was the Queen's bed-chamber, in which the Dauphin also slept; the second, which was separated from the Queen's by a small ante-chamber almost without light, was occupied by Madame Royale and Madame Elizabeth. This chamber was the only way to the turret-room on this story, and that turret-room was the only water-closet for this whole range of building, being in common for the Royal Family, the Municipal Officers, and the soldiers.

The King's apartments were on the third story. He slept in the great room, and made a study of the turret-closet. There was a kitchen separated from the King's chamber by a small dark room, which had been successively occupied by M. de Chamilly and M. Huë, and on which the seals were now fixed. The fourth

story was shut up; and on the ground floor there were
kitchens, of which no use was made.

The King usually rose at six in the morning: he
shaved himself, and I dressed his hair; he then went to
his reading-room, which being very small, the Municipal Officer on duty remained in the bedchamber with
the door open, that he might always keep the King in
sight. His Majesty continued praying on his knees for
five or six minutes, and then read till nine o'clock. In
that interval, after putting his chamber to rights, and
preparing the breakfast, I went down to the Queen,
who never opened her door till I arrived, in order to
prevent the Municipal Officer from going into her
apartment. I dressed the Prince and combed the
Queen's hair, then went and did the same for Madame
Royale and Madame Elizabeth. This service afforded
one of the opportunities I had of communicating to the
Queen and Princesses whatever I learnt; for when they
found by a sign that I had something to say, one of
them kept the Municipal Officer in talk, to divert his
attention.

At nine o'clock, the Queen, the children, and
Madame Elizabeth went up to the King's chamber to
breakfast, which having prepared for them, I put the
Queen and the Princesses' chambers to rights, with the
assistance of Tison and his wife, the only kind of work
in which they gave me any help. It was not for this
service only that these people were placed in the
Tower: a more important part was assigned them; they
were to observe whatever escaped the vigilance of
the Commissioners of the Municipality, and even to

inform against those Officers themselves. They were also doubtless intended to be made useful in the perpetration of whatever crimes might enter into the plan of those who had appointed them, for the woman, who then appeared of a mild disposition and stood in great awe of her husband, has since betrayed herself in an infamous accusation of the Queen,* at the conclusion of which she was seized with fits of madness. As for Tison, who had formerly been a custom-house officer of the lowest rank, he was an old fellow of a ferocious temper, incapable of pity, and a stranger to every sentiment of humanity. The Conspirators seemed determined to place the most vicious and degraded of mankind near the most virtuous and august.

At ten o'clock, the King and the Family went down to the Queen's chamber, and there passed the day. He employed himself in educating his Son, made him recite passages from Corneille and Racine, gave him lessons in geography, and exercised him in colouring the maps. The Prince's early quickness of apprehension fully repaid the fond cares of the King. He had so happy a memory that, on a map covered over with a blank sheet of paper, he could point out the departments, districts, towns, and courses of the rivers. It was the new geography of France,† which the King

---

* The unspeakable accusation brought against Marie Antoinette at her trial, that she was guilty of incest with her son.

† During the period of the Constituent Assembly, 1789–91, France was newly divided into eighty-three departments, and subdivided into districts, cantons, communes, whose officials were to be elected independently of the central authority.

taught him. The Queen, on her part, was employed in the education of her daughter; and these different lessons lasted till eleven o'clock. The remaining hour till noon was passed in needlework, knitting, or making tapestry. At noon, the Queen and Princesses retired to Madame Elizabeth's chamber, to change their dress: no Municipal Officer went in with them.

At one o'clock, when the weather was fine, the Royal Family were conducted to the garden by four Municipal Officers and the Commander of a legion of the National Guards. A great number of workmen being employed in the Temple, pulling down houses and raising new walls, the only walk allowed was a part of that under the great chestnut-trees. Being permitted to attend on these occasions, I engaged the young Prince to play, sometimes at football, sometimes at quoits, at running, and other active sports.

At two, we returned to the Tower, where I served the dinner: at which time Santerre the brewer, who was Commander in Chief of the National Guards of Paris, regularly came every day to the Temple, attended by two aides-de-camp. He minutely examined the different rooms; the King sometimes spoke to him, but the Queen never. After dinner the Royal Family withdrew to the Queen's chamber, where their Majesties usually played a party of piquet or trictrac; at which time I went to dinner.

At four o'clock, the King lay down for a few minutes, the Family, with books in their hands, sitting round him, and keeping profound silence while he slept. What a sight! a Monarch persecuted by hatred and calumny, fallen from his Throne into a prison, yet supported by the purity of his mind, and enjoying the peaceful slumbers of the good. . . . His consort, his children and his sister, with reverence contemplating his majestic countenance, whose serenity seemed to have increased with misfortune, and on which one might read by anticipation the bliss he now enjoys. . . . This sight will never be effaced from my memory.

On the King's waking, the conversation was resumed; and he would make me sit by him, while I taught his son to write. The copies I set were chosen by himself from the works of Montesquieu, and other celebrated authors. When this lesson was over, I attended the young Prince to Madame Elizabeth's chamber, where he played at ball or shuttle-cock.

In the evening, the Family sat round a table, while the Queen read to them from books of history, or other works proper to instruct and amuse her children, in which she often, unexpectedly, met with situations correspondent to her own, that gave birth to very afflicting reflections. Madame Elizabeth took the book in her turn, and in this manner they read till eight o'clock. I then gave the Prince his supper in Madame Elizabeth's chamber, during which the Family looked on, and the King took pleasure in diverting the children, by making them guess riddles in a collection of the *Mercures de France*, which he had found in the library.

After the Dauphin had supped, I undressed him, and the Queen heard him say his prayers: he said one in particular for the Princesse de Lamballe, and in

another he begged of GOD to protect the life of the
Marquise de Tourzel, his governess. When the Municipal Officers were too near, the Prince, of his own
accord, had the precaution to say these two prayers in
a low voice. We were out of their sight only two or
three minutes, just before I put him into bed, and if
I had anything to communicate to the Queen, I took
that opportunity. I acquainted her with the contents
of the journals, for though none of them were permitted in the Tower, a newsman, sent on purpose, used
to come every night at seven o'clock, and standing near
the wall by the side of the round Tower in the Temple
enclosure, cried, several times over, an account of all
that had been passing at the National Assembly, at the
Commune, and in the Armies. Placing myself in the
King's reading-room, I listened, and with the advan-
tage of perfect silence, remembered all I heard.

At nine, the King went to supper. The Queen and
Madame Elizabeth took it in turns to stay with the
Dauphin during this meal, and as I carried them whatever they wished from the table, it afforded me another
opportunity of speaking to them without witnesses.

After supper, the King went for a moment to the
Queen's chamber, shook hands with her and his sister
for the night, and kissed his children; then going to his
own apartment he retired to the turret-room, where he
sat reading till midnight. The Queen and the Princesses
locked themselves in. One of the Municipal Officers
remained in the little room which separated their
rooms, where he passed the night; the other followed
His Majesty.

I then made up my bed near the King's; but His Majesty, before he went to rest, waited to know who was the new Municipal Officer on duty, and if he had never seen him, commanded me to enquire his name. The Municipal Officers were relieved at eleven o'clock in the morning, five in the afternoon, and at midnight.

In this manner was the time passed as long as the King remained in the small Tower, which was till the thirtieth of September.

I SHALL now resume the order of events. On the fourth of September, Pétion's secretary came to the Tower to bring the King a sum of two thousand livres in assignats,* for which he obliged him to give a receipt. His Majesty requested him to pay M. Huë 526 livres, which he had advanced for his service, and he promised to do it. This sum of two thousand livres was the only payment made, notwithstanding the Legislative Assembly had voted 500,000 livres for His Majesty's expenses at the Tower of the Temple, though doubtless before they had suspected, or before they had dared to engage in, the real designs of their leaders.

Two days after, Madame Elizabeth desired me to collect some trifling things belonging to the Princesse de Lamballe, which she had left at the Tower when she was carried off. I made them up into a parcel, which

---

* *Assignats* were paper money whose value was based (*assigné*) on the property of the nation. They were created in 1789, and ceased to be issued in 1797.

I directed with a letter to her chief waiting-woman: and I have since learnt that neither the parcel nor the letter were ever delivered.

At this period, the characters of the greater part of the Municipal Officers picked out for the Temple showed what sort of men had been employed for the Revolution of the tenth of August, and for the massacres of the second of September.

One of them named James, a teacher of the English language, took it into his head one day to follow the King into his closet, and to sit down by him. His Majesty mildly told him that there his colleagues had always left him by himself, that as the door stood open he could never be out of his sight, but that the room was too small for two. James persisted in a harsh and brutal manner; the King was forced to submit, and giving up his course of reading for that day, returned to his chamber, where the Municipal Officer continued to beset him with the most tyrannical superintendence.

One morning when the King rose, he thought the Commissioner on duty was the same who had been upon guard the evening before, and expressed some concern that he had not been relieved; but this mark of goodness was only answered with insults. 'I come here', said the man, 'to watch your conduct, and not for you to busy yourself with mine.' Then going up close to His Majesty, with his hat on his head, he continued: 'Nobody has a right to meddle with it, and you less than anyone else.' He was insolent the whole day. I have since learnt that his name was Meunier.

Another Commissioner whose name was Le Clerc,

a physician, being in the Queen's chamber when I was teaching the Prince to write, interrupted him to pronounce a discourse on the republican education which it was necessary to give the Dauphin, and he wanted to change the books he was studying for works of the most revolutionary nature.

A fourth was present when the Queen was reading to her children from a volume of the History of France, at the period when the Constable de Bourbon took up arms against France. He pretended that the Queen meant by this to instil into the mind of her son ideas of vengeance against his Country, and laid a formal information against it before the Council. I warned Her Majesty about this, who afterwards selected subjects that could not be taken hold of to calumniate her intentions.

A man named Simon, shoemaker and Municipal Officer, was one of the six Commissioners appointed to inspect the works and expenses at the Temple*. He was the only one, who, under pretence of attending rigidly to his duty, never quitted the Tower. This man whenever he appeared in the presence of the Royal Family always treated them with the vilest insolence; he would frequently say to me close enough to the King to be heard by him: 'Cléry, ask Capet if he wants anything, that I mayn't have the trouble of coming up a second time.' I was obliged to answer that he wanted nothing. This is the same Simon to whose care the

* Antoine Simon was appointed concierge of the Temple prison, and after the King's death became guardian of the Dauphin. He was guillotined on the famous 10 *thermidor*.

4

young Louis was afterwards consigned, and who by a systematic barbarity prolonged the torments of that amiable and unfortunate child: there is also great reason to believe that he was the instrument made use of to shorten his days.

In teaching the young Prince to calculate I had made a multiplication table, according to directions given by the Queen. A Municipal Officer pretended that this was a means she took to teach her son how to correspond in code, and he was obliged to give up the study of arithmetic.

The same thing had happened with respect to the tapestry which the Queen and Madame Elizabeth had worked on their being first confined. Having finished some chair backs, the Queen ordered me to send them to the Duchesse de Sérent; but the Municipal Officers, whose leave I asked, thought that the designs contained hieroglyphics for the purpose of corresponding, and, in consequence, obtained an order, by which it was forbidden to suffer the works of the Queen and Princesses to be sent out of the Tower.

There were some of the Municipal Officers who never spoke of any of the Royal Family without the addition of the most insulting epithets. One of them named Turlot, one day said in my hearing: 'If no executioner could be found to guillotine this d—d family, I would guillotine them myself.'

When the King and Family went to walk they had to pass by a number of sentries, of which even at that period, there were several stationed within the small Tower. The soldiers on duty presented their arms to the Municipal Officers and Commanders of the Legions, but when the King approached them, they grounded their firelocks.

One of the soldiers within wrote one day on the King's chamber door, and that too on the inside: *The guillotine is permanent, and ready for the tyrant Louis XVI.* The King read the words, which I made an attempt to rub out, but His Majesty prevented me.

One of the door-keepers of the Tower, whose name was Rocher, a man of a horrid figure, accoutred as a pioneer, with long whiskers, a black hairy cap, a huge sabre, and a belt, to which hung a bunch of great keys, came up to the door when the King wanted to go out; he did not open it till His Majesty was quite close, and, pretending to search for the key among the many he had, which he rattled in a terrible manner, he designedly kept the Royal Family waiting, and then drew the bolts with a great clatter. After doing his, he ran down before them, and fixing himself on one side of the last door, with a long pipe in his mouth, puffed the fumes of his tobacco at each of the Royal Family as they went out, and most at the Queen and Princesses. Some National Guards, who were amused with these indignities, gathered round him, burst into fits of laughter at every puff of smoke, and used the grossest language; some of them went so far as to bring chairs from the guard-room to sit and enjoy the sight, obstructing the passage, of itself sufficiently narrow.

While the Family were walking, the artillerymen on guard danced and sang: their songs were always revolutionary, sometimes also obscene.

The same indignities were repeated on their return. The walls were frequently covered with the most indecent scrawls, in large letters, that they might not escape notice. Among others were—*Madame Véto shall swing**... *We shall find a way of bringing down the great hog's fat*... *Down with the red ribbon*†... *The little wolves must be strangled*... Under a gallows, with a figure hanging, were these words: *Louis taking an air bath*... and under a guillotine: *Louis spitting in the sack*,‡ or other similar ribaldry.

Thus was the short airing allowed to the Family turned into torture. This the King and Queen might have avoided by remaining within; but the air was necessary for their children, whom they most tenderly loved, and for their sakes it was that their Majesties daily endured, without complaining, these endless affronts.

A few instances, however, of fidelity or feeling occurred at times to soften the horror of these persecutions, and were the more striking from being uncommon.

---

* There had been much controversy in the Constituent Assembly as to whether to give the King an absolute veto over legislation. The constitution of 1791 gave the king a suspensive veto which could delay the implementation of the resolutions of the assembly for four years. The use the King made of this veto was very unpopular, and the mob nicknamed the King M. Véto and the Queen Mme. Véto.

† The ribbon of the Order of the Golden Fleece; see note on p. 61.

‡ *Crachant dans le sac*; this is a vulgar phrase alluding to the position of a person in the guillotine looking upon a little bag placed at the end to receive the head. (*Note to original edition.*)

As I was sitting alone reading in the antechamber next the Queen's room, the sentinel on guard at her door, an inhabitant of the suburbs, dressed neatly, but in plain country clothes, eyed me with much attention and appeared greatly moved. I got up to pass by him, on which he presented his arms, and, with a trembling voice, said: 'You must not go out.' 'Why not?' 'I am ordered to keep you in sight.' 'You are mistaken,' said I. 'What! Sir, are you not the King?' 'Don't you know him then?' 'I never saw him in my life, Sir; and wish, with all my heart, I could see him anywhere rather than here.' 'Speak low: I am going into that room, and will leave the door ajar, that you may see the King: he is sitting near the window, with a book in his hand.' I made the sentinel's wish known to the Queen; and the King, on her informing him of it, had the goodness to walk from one room to the other that he might have a view of him. When I went back 'Ah! Sir,' said he, 'how good is the King! how fond of his children!' He had seen him through the door caressing them, and was so affected as to be hardly able to speak. 'No,' continued he, striking his breast, 'I can never believe he has done us so much harm.' I here left him, fearing that his extreme agitation would betray him.

Another sentinel at the end of the walk, who was very young and had an interesting face, showed by his looks a desire to give the Royal Family some intelligence. Madame Elizabeth, in taking a second turn, went up to him, that he might have an opportunity of speaking; but whether through fear or respect,

he did not attempt it: his eyes, however, were full of
tears, and he made a sign that he had lodged a paper
in the rubbish, near the place where he was standing.
I went and looked for it, pretending to pick out stones
for the Prince to play with at quoits, but the Municipal
Officers coming up made me retire, and forbade me
ever again going so near the sentinels. I never knew
what were the intentions of this young man.

During the hour allowed for walking, another kind
of sight was presented to the Family that often
awakened their sensibility. Many of their faithful subjects, placing themselves at the windows of the houses
round the garden of the Temple, took the opportunity
of this short interval to see their King and Queen, and
it was impossible to be deceived in their sentiments
and their wishes. I once thought I could distinguish
the Marquise de Tourzel, and I was the more convinced
of it from the extreme attention with which the person
followed the Dauphin with her eyes, when he ran to
any distance from their Majesties. I made the observation to Madame Elizabeth, who could not refrain from
tears at the name of Madame de Tourzel, believing her
to be one of the victims of the second of September.
'What!' said she, 'can she be still alive?' The next
day, however, I found means to get information that
Madame de Tourzel was at one of her estates in the
country.

I found also that the Princesse de Tarente, and the
Marquise de la Roche-Aimon, who were at the Palace
of the Tuileries when it was attacked on the tenth of
August, had escaped the assassins. The safety of these

ladies, who on so many occasions had manifested their attachment, afforded the Royal Family some moments of consolation; but they very soon after heard the terrible news that the prisoners from the High Court of Orleans had been massacred on the ninth of September at Versailles. The King was overwhelmed with sorrow at the unhappy fate of the Duc de Brissac, who had not left his side for a single day since the beginning of the Revolution. His Majesty also grieved exceedingly for M. de Lessart, and the other interesting victims of their attachment to his person and their country.

O N the twenty-first of September, at four o'clock in the afternoon, one Lubin, a Municipal Officer, attended by horsemen and a great mob, came before the Tower to make a proclamation. Trumpets were sounded, and a dead silence ensued. Lubin's voice was of the Stentorian kind. The Royal Family could distinctly hear the proclamation of the abolition of Royalty, and of the establishment of a Republic. Hébert*, so well known by the name of

* Jacques René Hébert was one of the fortunately rare persons of whom nothing good can be said. Wholly uneducated, an atheist, and viciously cruel, he published a weekly paper, *Père Duchêne* (from which he took his nickname), that was directed against the King and the Royal Family, and was filthy both in its terms and its suggestions. It was Hébert who examined the little Dauphin and his sister in the Temple, forcing them to sign a document which they did not understand, of so obscene a nature that even Robespierre was revolted at it. In March, 1794, not realising that he himself was in danger, Hébert

Père du Chesne, and Destournelles, later Minister of Public Contributions, were then on guard over the Family: they were sitting at the time near the door, and stared the King in the face with a malicious grin. The Monarch perceived it, but, having a book in his hand, continued to read, without suffering the smallest alteration to appear upon his countenance. The Queen displayed equal resolution: not a word, not a gesture escaped either of them to increase the malignant enjoyment of those men. At the end of the proclamation the trumpets sounded again, and I went to one of the windows: the eyes of the populace were immediately turned upon me; I was taken for my Royal Master, and overwhelmed with abuse. The horsemen made menacing signs with their sabres, and I was obliged to withdraw to put an end to the tumult.

The same evening I informed the King that curtains and more clothes were wanting for the Dauphin's bed, as the weather began to be cold. He desired me to write the demand for them, which he signed. I used the same expressions I had hitherto done—*The King requires for his son*, and so forth. 'It is a great piece of assurance in you', said Destournelles, 'thus to use a title, abolished by the will of the people, as you have just heard.' I observed to him that I had heard a pro-

---

accused Danton in a speech at the Cordeliers of destroying freedom. Acting on this, Robespierre had Danton arrested, but within a few days Hébert also was dragged before the Revolutionary Tribunal, found guilty, and carried to the scaffold insensible. His wife, a former nun, followed him to the guillotine a few days later.

clamation, but was unacquainted with the object of it. 'It is', replied he, 'the abolition of Royalty and you may tell the gentleman', pointing to the King, 'to stop using a title no longer acknowledged by the people.' I told him I could not alter this note, which was already signed, as the King would ask me the reason, and it was not for me to tell it him. 'You will do as you like,' continued he, 'but I shall not certify the demand.' The next day, Madame Elizabeth gave me orders to write in future, for things of this kind, in the following style: *Such articles are wanted for the use of Louis XVI ... of Marie Antoinette ... of Louis Charles ... of Marie Thérèse ... of Marie Elizabeth.*

I had before been often under the necessity of repeating these demands. The small quantity of linen, brought to the Tower by the King and Queen, had been lent to them by some persons of the Court,* while they were at the Feuillants. Not any had been saved from the Tuileries, where on the fatal tenth of August all had been given up to pillage. Indeed, the Family was so much in want of clothes in general that the Princesses were employed in mending them every day, and Madame Elizabeth was often obliged to wait till the King was gone to bed, in order to have his to

* The Countess of Sutherland, Lady of the English Ambassador, found means to convey to the Queen some linen and other necessary articles for the young Prince. Her Majesty ordered me afterwards to send them back to the Countess, desiring me to write a letter, on her part, expressing her thanks; the Queen being at that time debarred from ink and paper. The Municipal Officers, however, would not allow them to be sent, but kept the linen and the other things. (*Note by Cléry.*)

repair. At last, after many applications, I obtained the
grant of a little new linen, but the sempstresses having
marked it with crowns above the letters, the Municipal
Officers insisted upon the Princesses picking out the
crowns: and they were forced to obey.

On the twenty-sixth of September, I learnt, through
a Member of the Municipality, that it was intended to
separate the King from his Family, and that the apartment preparing for him in the great Tower would soon
be ready. I broke this new tyranny to the King in the
most wary manner possible, and expressed how much
I had felt at being forced to afflict him. 'You cannot',
said His Majesty, 'give me a greater proof of your
attachment; I require it of your affection that you
should hide nothing from me, for I am prepared for
anything: endeavour to gain intelligence of the day
when this painful separation is to take place, and let me
know it.'

On the twenty-ninth of September, at ten o'clock in
the morning, five or six Municipal Officers walked into
the Queen's chamber, where the Royal Family were
assembled. One of them, whose name was Char-
bonnier, read to the King a decree of the Council,
ordering that 'paper, pens, ink, pencils, knives, and
even papers written upon, whether found on the
persons of the prisoners, or in their rooms, or on the
valet de chambre, or others serving in the Tower,
should be taken away.' 'And whenever', added he
from himself, 'you may want anything, Cléry may go
down and write what you require in a register that
will be kept in the Council Chamber.' The King and

the whole Family gave up their papers, pencils, and the contents of their pockets, without making a reply. The Commissioners then searched the rooms and closets, and took away the things pointed out by the decree. I now learnt from a Member of this deputation that on that very night the King was to be removed to the great Tower, and I found means of informing His Majesty of this by Madame Elizabeth.

In fact, after supper, as the King was leaving the Queen's chamber to go up to his own, a Municipal Officer bade him stop, the Council having something to communicate to him. A quarter of an hour afterwards, the six Officers, who in the morning had taken away the papers, came in and read a second decree of the Commune to the King, ordering his removal to the great Tower. Although prepared for this event, he was again affected in the most lively manner: his disconsolate Family endeavoured to read in the looks of the Commissioners how far their designs were intended to be carried. The King left them in the most cruel state of alarm at bidding him adieu, and this separation, which portended so many other calamities, was the most cruel suffering their Majesties had hitherto experienced in the Temple. I attended the King to his new prison.

THE King's apartment in the great Tower was not finished. A solitary bed was its only furniture. The painters and paper-hangers were still at work in it, which left an insufferable smell, and I feared this would have incommoded His Majesty. The room intended for me was at a very great distance from the King's. I begged most earnestly to be placed near him, and passed the first night in a chair by his bedside. The next day the King prevailed, though with much difficulty, to get me a room contiguous to his own.

After His Majesty had risen, I wanted to go to the small Tower to dress the Prince, but the Municipal Officers objected. One of them whose name was Véron, said to me: 'You are to have no more communication with the prisoners, nor is your master either; he is not even to see his children again.'

At nine o'clock, the King desired to be shown to his Family. 'We have no such orders', said the Commissioners. His Majesty made some observations, to which they gave no answer.

Half an hour afterwards two Municipal Officers came in, followed by a servant boy, who brought the King a roll and a small carafe of lemonade for his breakfast. His Majesty expressed his desire to dine with his Family. They answered that they would apply to the Commune for orders. 'But', added the King, 'let my valet de chambre go down, he has the care of my son, and there can be no reason to prevent his continuing to attend upon him.' 'That does not depend upon us', said the Commissioners, and went away.

I was then in a corner of the chamber, overwhelmed with grief, and absorbed in the most heart-rending reflections on the lot of this august Family. On one hand, I saw before me the pangs of my Royal Master, and on the other, I represented to myself the young Prince delivered over, perhaps, to strange hands. It had already been said that he was to be taken from their Majesties, and what fresh tortures would not such a separation occasion to the Queen? I was engrossed with these painful ideas, when the King came up to me, with the roll, that had been brought him, in his hand. He presented half of it to me, saying: 'It seems they have forgotten your breakfast; take this: the remainder is enough for me.' I excused myself, but he insisted upon it. It was impossible for me to restrain my tears; the King perceived it, and gave way to his own.

At ten o'clock, some other Members of the Municipality brought the workmen to continue their employment in the room. One of these Officers told the King that he had just been present while the Family were at breakfast, and that they were very well. 'I thank you,' replied the King, 'pray remember me to them, and say, that I too am well. May I not', added he, 'have some books which I left in the Queen's room? I would thank you for them, as I have nothing to read.' His Majesty described the books he wanted, and the Officer complied with his request, but not being able to read, he desired I would go with him. I congratulated myself on this man's ignorance, and blessed Providence for this consolatory moment. The King gave me some orders, and his looks spoke the rest.

I found the Queen in her chamber, with her children and Madame Elizabeth about her. They were all weeping, and their grief increased on seeing me. They immediately asked me a thousand questions about the King, which I was forced to answer with reserve. The Queen, addressing the Officers who had accompanied me, again urged her request of being permitted to see the King, if it were but for a few moments in the day, and at their meals. It was no question simply of complaints and tears, but of anguished entreaty. 'Well, they *shall* dine together to-day,' said one of the Officers, 'but as we must be ruled by the decrees of the Commune, we will act to-morrow according as they shall prescribe.' To this his associates consented.

At the very idea of being again with the King, a sensation, almost amounting to joy, seemed to re-animate this unfortunate Family. The Queen, folding her children in her arms, and Madame Elizabeth, raising her hands to Heaven, thanked G O D for the unlooked-for happiness. It was a most affecting sight. Even some of the Municipal Officers could not refrain from tears (they were the only tears I ever saw shed by any of them in this horrid abode). One of them, it was Simon the shoemaker, said, loud enough to be heard: 'I believe these b—s of women would make *me* cry.' Then, turning to the Queen, he added: 'When you were assassinating the people on the tenth of August, you did not cry at all.' 'The people', replied the Queen, 'are grossly deceived as to our feelings.'

I then took the books which the King had desired to have, and carried them to him; the Municipal Officers accompanying me, to let His Majesty know that he should be allowed to see his Family. I remarked that I should no doubt continue to wait upon the Queen, the Dauphin and Princesses: they consented. I thus had an opportunity of informing Her Majesty of what had passed, and all that the King had suffered since he left her.

Dinner was served in the King's room, whither the Family repaired, and it was easy to judge of the fears that had agitated their minds, by the emotions that burst forth on this meeting. Nothing more was heard of the decree of the Commune, and His Majesty continued not only to meet his Family at meals, but to join them in their walks.

After dinner, the Queen was shown the apartment preparing for her above the King's: she entreated the workmen to finish it quickly, but they were three weeks longer at work upon it.

IN that interval, I continued my attendance on their Majesties, and also on the Dauphin and the Princesses: they spent their time much in the same way as before. The King's attention to the education of his son met with no interruption; but the Royal Family's residing thus in two separate Towers, by rendering the superintendence of the Municipal Officers more difficult, rendered them also more vigilant. The number of the Municipal Officers was augmented, and their jealousy left me very few means of getting intelligence of what was passing abroad: the following were the methods I took for that purpose.

Under pretence of having linen and other necessary articles brought me, I obtained permission that my wife should come to the Temple once a week: she was always accompanied by one of her friends, a lady who passed for her relation. Nobody could evince greater attachment for the Royal Family than did this lady, by her actions, and by the risks she ran on several occasions. On their arrival, I was called down to the Council Chamber, where, however, I could speak to them only in the presence of the Municipal Officers: we were closely watched, and at several of the first visits I could not find an opportunity to my purpose. I then gave them to understand that they should come at one o'clock: that was the hour of walking, during which the greater part of the Municipal Officers were following the Royal Family: there used then to be but one of them remaining in the Council Chamber, and when this happened to be a civil man, he left us a little more at liberty, still, however, without losing sight of us.

Having thus an opportunity of speaking without being overheard, I made enquiries respecting those for whom the Royal Family interested themselves, and gained information of what was passing at the Convention. The circumstance of the newsman, whom I have mentioned, proved to be a project of my wife's, who had employed him to come every day under the walls of the Temple, and cry repeatedly the contents of the Journals.

In addition to my intelligence thus obtained, I contrived to procure a little more from some of the Officers

'The Royal Family walking in the garden of the Temple, while Cléry plays ball with the Dauphin'

themselves, and I was particularly assisted by a person of great fidelity, whose name was Turgy,* a Groom of the King's kitchen, who, from attachment to His Majesty, had found means of getting himself employed at the Temple, with two of his comrades, Marchand and Chrétien. These two brought the dishes for the table of the Royal Family, dressed in a kitchen at a considerable distance; they were also employed in marketing, and Turgy, who shared that office with them, going out of the Temple in his turn twice or thrice a week, had it in his power to gain information of what was passing. The difficulty was how I should be made acquainted with it; for he was forbidden to speak to me except upon his business, and that always in presence of the Municipal Officers. When he had anything to say, he made me a sign agreed upon, and I then strove to detain him under various pretexts. Sometimes I begged him to dress my hair, during which Madame Elizabeth, who knew of my understanding with Turgy, kept the Municipal Officers talking, so that I had time enough for our conversations: sometimes I contrived an opportunity of his going to my chamber, of which he availed himself to put the

* Louis François Turgy was born in Paris in 1763, and at the age of twenty-one entered the royal household. He became one of the King's most devoted servants, and it was by his means that Louis was able to correspond with the Queen and Princess Elizabeth. After the King's death, he followed Madame Royale to Vienna, and to the different places in which she took up residence. At the Restoration Louis XVIII conferred on him letters of nobility, and made him an Officer of the Legion of Honour. He died in Paris in 1823.

Journals, Memoirs, and other publications he had for me, under my bed.

When the King or the Queen wished for intelligence, if the day of my wife's coming happened to be distant, I gave the commission to Turgy. If it was not his turn to go out, I pretended to want something for the use of the Royal Family: on which he would reply 'Another day will do.' 'Very well,' I used to answer, with an air of indifference, 'the King will wait.' My object was to induce the Municipal Officers to order him out, which frequently happened, and then the same evening or next morning, he gave me the particulars I wanted. We had agreed upon this mode of understanding one another, but took care not to repeat the same methods before the same Commissioners.

Still fresh obstacles were to be surmounted before I could impart the intelligence to the King. The only time I had to speak to him was when they were relieving the Municipal Officers, and as he went to bed. Sometimes, I caught a moment in the morning, before the Commissioners were ready to make their appearance. I pretended not to want to go in till they did, while making them realise that His Majesty was waiting for me. If they allowed me to go in, I immediately drew his curtains, and while I put on his stockings and shoes, spoke without being seen or heard: but I was more frequently disappointed in my hope, for the Municipal Officers generally compelled me to stay till they were dressed, that they might go with me into His Majesty's room. Several of them treated me with harshness: some ordered me in the morning to remove their beds, and forced me at night to bring them back; others were incessantly taunting me: but this conduct afforded me fresh means of being useful to their Majesties. By returning only mildness and civility I gained upon them in spite of their natures, and infusing a confidence into their minds, unperceived by themselves, I often managed to collect even from *them* the information I wanted.

Such was the plan I had been pursuing with the greatest caution from my arrival at the Temple, when an event as extraordinary as unexpected made me fear that I should be for ever separated from the Royal Family.

One evening, about six o'clock, it was the fifth of October, after having seen the Queen to her apartment, I was returning to the King's with two Municipal Officers, when the sentinel at the guard-room door, taking me by the arm, and calling me by my name, asked me how I did, and said with an air of mystery that he wished very much to speak to me. 'Sir,' cried I, 'speak out; I am not allowed to whisper with anybody.' 'I was assured', replied the sentinel, 'that the King had lately been thrown into a dungeon, and you with him.' 'You see it is not so,' said I; and left him. There was one Officer walking before and another behind me. the former stopped and heard us.

Next morning, two Commissioners waited for me at the door of the Queen's apartment: they conducted me to the Council Chamber, where I was examined by the Municipal Officers there assembled. I reported the conversation exactly as it had passed, which was confirmed by the Officer who had heard it: the other alleged that the sentinel had given me a paper, that he had heard the rumpling of it, and that it was a letter for the King. I denied the fact, desiring they would search me, and take all means of satisfying themselves. A minute of the sitting of the Council was drawn up; I was confronted with the sentinel, who was sentenced to be confined for four and twenty hours.

I supposed this affair at an end, when, on the twenty-sixth of October, while the Royal Family were at dinner, a Municipal Officer walked in, followed by six soldiers with drawn sabres, together with a Clerk of the Rolls, and a tipstaff, both in their official dress. I was terrified lest they should be come for the King. The Royal Family all rose, and the King asked what they wanted with him, but the Officer, without replying, called me into another room: the soldiers followed us, and the clerk having read a warrant to arrest me, I was seized in order to be taken before the tribunal. I begged permission to inform the King of it, and was answered that I was no longer at liberty to speak to him. 'But you may take a shirt,' added the Officer, 'it won't be a long business.' I thought I understood him, and took only my hat. I passed by the King and the Royal Family, who were standing, and in consternation at the manner in which I was taken away. The populace assembled in the Temple Court heaped abuse upon me, calling out for my head. They were told by one of the National Guards that it was necessary to save my life, in order to discover secrets which I alone knew. The same vociferations, however, continued all the way.

The moment we arrived at the Palais de Justice, I was confined alone; there I remained six hours, endeavouring in vain to find out what could be the motives for my being arrested. All I could bring to my mind was that on the morning of the tenth of August, during the attack on the Tuileries, some persons, who were trapped there and wished to make their way out, begged me to hide several valuable articles and papers that might have betrayed them, in a chest of drawers that belonged to me: I suspected that these papers had been seized, and would now, perhaps, cost me my life.

At eight o'clock, I appeared before the Judges, who were unknown to me. This was a revolutionary tribunal, established on the seventeenth of August, in order to select, among those who had escaped the fury of the populace, such as were doomed to die. What was my astonishment when I saw, among the prisoners to be tried, the very young man who was suspected of having given me a letter three weeks before, and when I found my accuser to be the Municipal Officer who had already denounced me to the Council at the Temple! I was examined, witnesses were produced, and the Municipal Officer repeated his accusation. I told him he was unworthy of being a Magistrate of the People; that as he had heard the rumpling of the paper, and thought I had received a letter, he should immediately have had me searched, instead of staying eighteen hours before he lodged any information whatever. The arguments being concluded, the Jury consulted together, and on their verdict we were acquitted. The President charged four Municipal Officers, who were present at my acquittal, to conduct me back to the Temple. It was twelve o'clock at night, and we arrived just as the King was gone to bed, to whom I was permitted to make my return known. The Royal Family had been very much concerned at my fate, not doubting but that I had already been condemned.

It was at this juncture that the Queen took possession of the apartment that was prepared for her in the great Tower: but even this longed-for day, that seemed to promise their Majesties some comfort, was distinguished, on the part of the Municipal Officers, by a fresh mark of their animosity against the Queen. From the hour of her being brought to the Temple they had seen her devoting her life to the care of her son, and in his gratitude and caresses finding some alleviation to her wretchedness: they took him from her, and that without any previous notice. Her affliction was extreme. The young Prince, however, was placed with the King, and the care of him given to me. How pathetically did the Queen charge me to be watchful over his life!

As the events which I shall have to speak of in future, occurred in a place situated differently from that which I have before described, I think it will be proper here to give also a description of their Majesties' new habitation.

THE great Tower is about a hundred and fifty feet high, and consists of four stories, arched and supported in the middle by a great pillar from the bottom to the top. The area within the walls was about thirty feet square.

The second and third stories allotted to the Royal Family, being, as were all the other stories, single rooms, they were now each divided into four chambers by partitions of board. The ground floor was for the use of the Municipal Officers; the first story was kept as a guard-room; the King was lodged in the second.

The first room of his apartments was an antechamber (1), from which three doors led to three separate rooms. Opposite the entrance was the King's chamber (2), in which a bed was placed for the Dauphin: mine was on the left (3), so was the dining-room (4), which was divided from the antechamber by a glazed partition. There was a chimney in the King's chamber: the other rooms were warmed by a great stove in the antechamber. The light was admitted into each of these rooms by windows, but these were blocked up with great iron bars, and slanting screens on the outside, which prevented a free circulation of the air: the embrasures of the windows were nine feet thick.

Every story of the great Tower communicated with four turrets, built at the angles.

In one of these turrets was a staircase (5) that went up as far as the battlements, and on which wickets were placed at certain distances to the number of seven. This staircase opened on every floor through two gates: the first of oak, very thick and studded with nails, the second of iron.

Another of the turrets (6) formed a closet to the King's chamber; the third served for a water-closet (7), and in the fourth (8) was kept the firewood, where also the temporary beds, on which the Municipal Officers slept near the King, were deposited in the daytime.

The four rooms, of which the King's apartments consisted, had a false ceiling of cloth, and the partitions were hung with wallpaper. The antechamber had the appearance of the interior of a jail, and on one of the panels was hung the Declaration of the Rights of Man, in very large characters with a tricolor border. A chest of drawers, a small bureau, four chairs with cushions, an arm-chair, a few rush-bottomed chairs, a table, a glass over the chimney, and a green damask bed, were all the furniture of the King's chamber: these articles, as well as what was in the other rooms, were taken from the Temple Palace. The King's bed was that in which the Comte d'Artois' Captain of the Guards used to sleep.*

The Queen occupied the third story, which was arranged in much the same manner as the King's. The bedchamber for the Queen and Madame Royale (9), was above His Majesty's: in the turret (10) was their

---

* The Duc d'Angoulême, as Grand Prior of France, was proprietor of the Temple Palace. The Comte d'Artois had furnished it, and made it his residence when he came to Paris. The great Tower, about two hundred paces from the Palace, and standing in the middle of the garden, was the depository of the archives of the Order of Malta. (*Note to original edition.*)

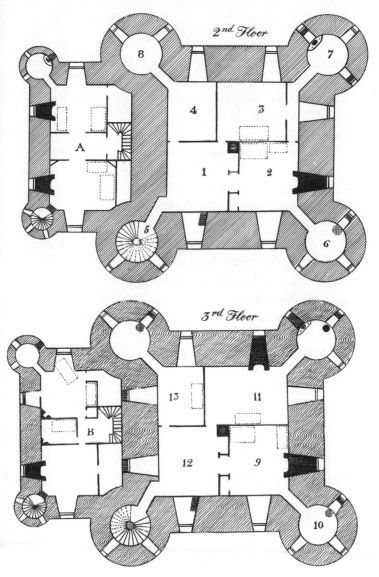

Plan of the Tower of the Temple.

closet. Madame Elizabeth's room (11) was over mine. The entrance served for an antechamber (12), where the Municipal Officers watched by day and slept at night. Tison and his wife were lodged over the King's dining-room. (13)

The fourth story was not occupied. A gallery ran all along within the battlements which sometimes served as a walk. The embrasures were stopped up with blinds to prevent the Family from seeing or being seen.

Few changes were made, after their Majesties were reunited in the great Tower, as to the hours of their meals, their reading, their walks, or as to the time they had hitherto dedicated to the education of their children. Soon after the King was up, he read the form of prayer of the Knights of the Holy Ghost,* and as Mass had not been permitted at the Temple, even on holidays, he commanded me to purchase a breviary, such as was used in the Diocese of Paris. This Monarch was of a religious turn, but his religion, pure and enlightened, never encroached upon his other duties. Books of travels, Montesquieu's works, those of Buffon, de Pluche's *Spectacle de la Nature*, Hume's *History of England*, in English, *On the Imitation of Christ*, in Latin, Tasso, in Italian, and French Plays, were what he usually read from his first being sent into confinement. He devoted four hours a day to Latin authors.†

* See note on p. 61.

† 'As soon as dinner was finished, the King customarily went into the library of the Archives of the Order of Malta, which

The Queen and Madame Elizabeth having desired books of devotion similar to those of the King, His Majesty commanded me to purchase them. Often have I seen Madame Elizabeth on her knees by her bed-side praying with fervency.

At nine o'clock, the King and his son were summoned to breakfast: I attended them. I afterwards dressed the hair of the Queen and Princesses, and, by the Queen's orders, taught Madame Royale to dress hair. While I was doing this the King played at drafts or chess, sometimes with the Queen, sometimes with Madame Elizabeth.

After dinner, the Dauphin and his sister went into the antechamber to play at battledore and shuttle-cock, at Siam,* or some other game. Madame Elizabeth was always with them, and generally sat at a table with a book in her hand. I stayed with them too, and sometimes read, at which time I sat down in obedience to

---

formerly occupied the tower. The books were still on the shelves, and His Majesty used to choose some of them to read. One day when I was there with the King, he pointed to the works of Rousseau and Voltaire. "These two men", he said to me in a whisper, "have caused the ruin of France." In the hope of regaining his former ease in reading Latin, and of being able, during his imprisonment, to give the Dauphin his first lessons in that language, the King translated the *Odes* of Horace, and parts of Cicero' (M. Huë).

* The game of Siam is played on a board, with a bowl and twelve or thirteen small wooden pins. The bowl is flattened, and cut in such a manner that by rolling it on the edge it always makes a circle that gradually diminishes, and it throws down the pins which are set up in a ring. (*Note to original edition.*)

her orders. This dispersion of the Royal Family often perplexed the two Municipal Officers on guard, who, anxious not to leave the King and Queen alone, were still more so not to leave one another, so great was their mutual distrust. This was the time Madame Elizabeth took to ask me questions or give me orders. I both listened to her and answered, without taking my eyes from the book in my hand, that I might not be surprised by the Municipal Officers. The Dauphin and Madame Royale, instructed by their aunt, facilitated these conversations, by being noisy in their play, and often made signs to her that the Officers were coming. I found it necessary to be particularly cautious of Tison, dreaded as he was even by the Commissioners, whom he had several times denounced: the King and Queen too treated him with kindness in vain; nothing could subdue his innate malignity.

At night, after bedtime, the Municipal Officers ranged their beds in the antechamber in such a manner as to block up His Majesty's door. They also locked one of the doors in my room, by which I could have gone into the King's, and took away the key, so that if His Majesty happened to call me in the night, I was forced to pass through the antechamber, bear their ill-humour, and wait till they chose to get up.

O N the seventh of October, at six o'clock at night, I was summoned to the Council Chamber, where I found a score of Municipal Officers, with Manuel as President, who, from being Solicitor to the Commune, was become a Member of the National Convention: the sight of him surprised and alarmed me. I was directed to remove, that very night, the Orders still worn by the King, such as those of St Louis and the Golden Fleece: His Majesty no longer wore that of the Holy Ghost, which had been suppressed by the first Assembly.*

I represented that I could not do it, and that it was not my part to make the decrees of the Council known to the King. I hoped by this to gain time to break it to His Majesty, and I perceived besides, by their embarrassment, that they were then acting without the authority of any decree either of the Convention or the Commune. The Commissioners were unwilling to go up to the King, till Manuel determined them by offering to go with them. The King was seated, and engaged in reading. Manuel spoke first, and the conversation which followed was as remarkable for the indecent familiarity of the Deputy, as for the temper and serenity of the Monarch.

'How do you find yourself?' said Manuel, 'have you everything you want?' 'I content myself with what I have', replied His Majesty. 'No doubt you have heard of the victories gained by our armies, of the

---

* The *Toison d'Or*, or Golden Fleece, was the chief Austrian and Spanish Order, founded in the fifteenth century at Bruges by Philip the Good, Duke of Burgundy. The Order of St Louis was an order of military merit, and was founded by Louis XIV. The Order of the Holy Ghost, the famous *Cordon Bleu*, though not the oldest French Order, was the chief; every 'Son of France' was automatically a Knight of this Order from his birth,

taking of Spires, of Nice, and of the conquest of Savoy?' 'I heard it mentioned some days ago, by one of those gentlemen, who was reading the *Journal du Soir*.' 'What! don't you get the Journals, that are become so interesting?' 'I never receive any of them.' 'Oh! Sirs,' said Manuel, turning to the Municipal Officers, and pointing to the King, 'you must let the gentleman have the Journals; it is right he should be informed of our successes.' Then, again addressing His Majesty, 'Democratic principles are spreading: you know that the people have abolished Royalty, and adopted the Republican form of government.' 'I have heard it, and I pray to GOD that the French people may be as happy as I have always wished to make them.' 'You know too that the National Assembly has suppressed all Orders of Chivalry: you ought to have been told to leave off the ornaments of them: returned to the class of other citizens, you must expect to be treated like others; with this exception, ask for whatever you want, it shall be immediately procured for you.' 'I thank you,' said the King, 'I want nothing.' His Majesty here returned to his book; and Manuel, who had been endeavouring to discover vexation, or provoke impatience in him, had the mortification of finding only a noble resignation, and an unalterable composure.

The deputation now withdrew, and one of the Officers desired me to follow him to the Council Chamber, where I was again ordered to take the ornaments from the King's person. Manuel added: 'You will do well to send the crosses and ribbons to the Convention. I must also inform you', continued he 'that Louis' confinement may last a long while, and that if it be not your intention to remain here, you had better take this opportunity of declaring it. It is also in contemplation, in order to render the superintendence more easy, to decrease the number of people employed in the Tower. If you stay with the late King, you will be left entirely by yourself, and you must expect hard work: wood and water will be brought you once a week, but it will be your business to clean the rooms, and do the rest of the work.' I replied, that being determined never to forsake my Master, I would submit to everything. I was conducted back to His Majesty's chamber, who said to me: 'You heard what passed with those gentlemen, I would have you to-night take off the Orders from my coats.'

The next morning, when I was dressing the King, I told him that I had locked up the crosses and ribbons, although Manuel had given me to understand that it would be proper to send them to the Convention. 'You have done right', replied His Majesty.

It has been reported that Manuel came to the Temple, in the month of September, to prevail upon His Majesty to write to the King of Prussia, at the time he marched his army into Champagne. I can testify that Manuel came but twice to the Temple while I was there, first, on the third of September, then on the seventh of October; that each time he was accompanied by a great number of Municipal Officers, and that he never had any private conversation with the King.

6

On the ninth of October, a Journal of the debates of the Convention was brought to the King, but some days after a Municipal Officer, whose name was Michel, a perfumer, obtained a decree again prohibiting the admission of the public papers into the Tower. He sent for me to the Council Chamber, and asked me by what authority I had ordered the Journals to be addressed to me. In reality, without my knowing anything of it, four Journals had every day been brought, with this direction printed: *To the valet de chambre of Louis XVI at the Tower of the Temple.* I could not find out, and am still ignorant, who paid the subscription for them. Michel, however, wanted to force me to tell who they were, and made me write to the editors of the Journals for information, but their answers, if they sent any, were never communicated to me.

This prohibition, however, of the Journals being admitted into the Tower, had its exceptions when these papers furnished opportunities of new insults. If they contained abusive expressions against the King or Queen, atrocious threats or infamous calumnies, some Municipal Officer or other was sure, with studied malice, to place them on the chimney-piece, or on the chest of drawers in His Majesty's chamber, that they might fall into his hands.

He once read in one of those papers the petition of an artilleryman for the head of the tyrant Louis XVI, that he might load his piece with it, and shoot it at the enemy. Another Journal, speaking of Madame Elizabeth, and endeavouring to destroy the admiration she

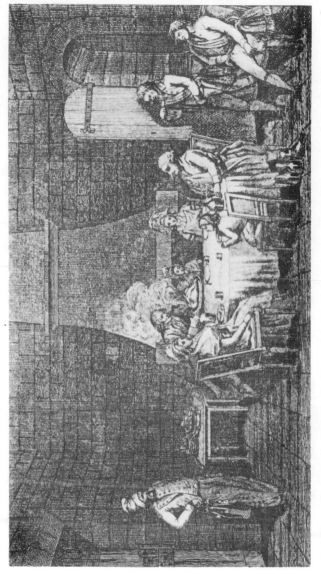

Louis Capet dines with his family in the Tower of the Temple in the presence of the Gaoler and two municipal officers, one of whom is taking out his watch and announcing that it is time for the ladies to retire'

had excited in the public, by the noble manner in which she had devoted herself to the King and Queen, asserted that virtuous Princess to have had a child by a Bishop, adding, that this young wolf ought to be smothered, with the two others in the Tower, meaning the Dauphin and Madame Royale.

These articles affected the King only for the sake of the people. 'How very unfortunate are the French', said he, 'to suffer themselves to be imposed upon in this manner.' If I saw these Journals first, I took care to remove them out of His Majesty's way; but they were frequently brought in when I was employed elsewhere, so that very few of the articles written for the purpose of abusing the Royal Family, whether to exite the populace to regicide, or to prepare the minds of the people to suffer its being perpetrated, were not read by the King. They only who remember the insolent writings that were published at that time can have an idea of this kind of unprecedented torture.

The influence of these sanguinary writings was also observable in the conduct of such of the Municipal Officers as had not before shown themselves so hard-hearted or distrustful as others.

One day after dinner, having just written an account of expenses in the Council Chamber, I had locked it up in a desk of which they had given me the key. My back was scarcely turned, when Marinot, a Municipal Officer, said to his colleagues, though he was not on duty, that they ought to open the desk, and examine its contents, to ascertain whether or not I had a correspondence with the enemies of the people. 'I know him well', added he, 'and am sure he receives letters for the King.' Then accusing his colleages of remissness, he abused them violently, threatened to impeach them all before the Council of the Commune as accomplices, and went out to put his threat into execution. A minute was immediately drawn up of all the papers in the desk, and sent to the Commune, where Marinot had already laid his information.

Another day, on seeing a draught-board, which with the permission of his colleagues I had sent to be mended, brought back, he pretended it might contain a letter, had it entirely taken to pieces, and when he found nothing, made the workmen paste it together again before his eyes.

Once, my wife and her friend coming to the Tower as usual on a Thursday, I was speaking with them in the Council Chamber, when the Queen and Madame Elizabeth, who were walking, saw us, and nodded to us. This notice of mere affability was observed by Marinot, and it was ground enough for him to have my wife and her friend arrested as they were going out of the Council Chamber. They were examined separately: my wife being asked who the lady was that accompanied her, declared she was her sister, while to the same question the other had replied that they were cousins. This contradiction furnished subject for a long written statement, and the most serious suspicions, Marinot pretending that this lady was one of the Queen's Pages in disguise. However, after a most painful and insulting examination, that lasted three hours, they were set at liberty.

They were still permitted to come to the Tower, but we redoubled our caution. I had often in those short interviews managed to slip into their hands notes written with a pencil, which had escaped the searches of the Municipal Officers, and which I concealed with great care. These notes related to some information their Majesties wished to have: luckily on that day they had not received any; if one had been found upon them, we should all three have been in the greatest danger.

There were others of the Municipal Officers who had the most extravagant whims. One ordered some macaroons to be broken to see if there was no letter concealed in them. Another, on the same pretence, had some peaches cut before him, and the stones cracked. A third one day compelled me to drink the liquid soap prepared for shaving the King, affecting to apprehend it was poison. After dinner and supper, Madame Elizabeth used to give me a gold-bladed knife to clean, which the Municipal Officer would often snatch out of my hand, to examine if I had not slipped some paper into the sheath.

Madame Elizabeth having commanded me to send a book of devotion to the Duchesse de Sérent, the Municipal Officers cut off the margins, for fear anything should have been written upon them with a secret ink.

One of them one day forbade my going up to the Queen to dress her hair: Her Majesty was to come down to the King's apartments, and to bring her powder and combs herself.

Another would follow her into Madame Elizabeth's chamber to see her change her clothes, which she usually did at noon: I represented to him the indecency of such behaviour, but he persisted, and Her Majesty was obliged to give up dressing, and leave the room.

When the linen was brought from the wash, the Officers made me unfold it article by article, and examined it always by daylight. The washerwoman's book, and every paper used for packing, were held to the fire, to ascertain whether there were not any secret writing upon them. The linen worn by the King, Queen, Prince, and Princesses, was in like manner examined.

There were, however, some of the Municipal Officers who were not so hardened as their colleagues; but most of these, becoming suspected by the Committee of Public Safety, have fallen victims to their humanity, and those who are still alive have been long groaning in confinement.

A young man called Toulan, whom by his manner of speaking I thought to be one of the greatest enemies of the Royal Family, came up to me one day, and pressing my hand, said with an air of mystery: 'I can't speak to the Queen to-day, on account of my comrades; let her know that I have executed her commission, that in a few days I shall be on duty, and that I will then bring her an answer.' Amazed on hearing him speak thus, and fearing that he was laying a snare for me, I answered that he was mistaken in addressing himself to me on such errands. 'No, I am not mistaken', replied he, pressing my hand with still more warmth, and retiring. On my informing the Queen of this conversation, she told me I might trust Toulan. This young man was afterwards involved on Her Majesty's trial, with nine other Municipal Officers, accused of having agreed to favour her escape at the time she was at the Temple. Toulan was put to death.

THEIR Majesties, for the three months that they had now been shut up in the Tower, had been accustomed to the sight only of Municipal Officers, when on the first of November, a deputation from the National Convention was announced to them. This deputation consisted of Drouet,* the Post-Master at Varennes, Chabot, formerly a Capuchin,† Dubois-Crancé,‡ Duprat and two others whose names I do

---

* Jean Baptiste Drouet was the postmaster at Varennes, to whom it was largely due that the Royal Family were recognised during their attempted flight, and brought back to Paris.

† François Chabot, a Capuchin and Constitutional Bishop. He was a member of the National Convention, and was guillotined under the Terror.

‡ Edmond Louis Alexis Dubois de Crancé joined the party of Danton in the Assembly, and was one of the most bigoted of the King's enemies. After voting for his death, he was appointed President of the Assembly, and a member of the Committee of Public Safety. Despite this, he was later accused of being too moderate, and arrested, but shortly released. Under the Directory, Dubois was Minister of War, but when Napoleon became Consul he opposed him, a fact which resulted in his compulsory retirement. He then took on the editorship of *L'Ami des Lois* until Napoleon was appointed Life Consul, after which he left public life altogether, and died at his property in Champagne at an advanced age.

not recollect. The Royal Family, and particularly the Queen, shuddered with horror at the sight of Drouet, who insolently seated himself by her: Chabot, following his example, also took a chair. They asked the King how he was treated, and if he was supplied with necessaries. 'I complain of nothing', replied His Majesty, 'and only request that the Committee will supply my valet de chambre with 2000 livres, or leave it with the Council, to defray the small current expenses, and that we may have some linen and other clothes, of which we are in the greatest need.' The Deputies promised it should be attended to, but nothing was sent.

Some days after, the King caught a great cold in his head, on which I requested that M. Dubois, His Majesty's Dentist, might be sent for. It was debated for three days, and at last refused. A fever coming on, His Majesty was permitted to consult M. le Monnier,* his chief Physician. It would be difficult to paint the grief of this venerable old man when he saw his Master.

The Queen and her Children never left the King during the day, waited upon him with me, and often assisted me to make his bed. At night, I sat up alone with His Majesty. M. le Monnier came twice a day,

---

* Louis Guillaume Lemonnier, Chief Medical Officer to the Army, Physician to the Children of France, and later, Physician in Ordinary to Louis XVI, was born in 1717, and thus was already elderly when called in to see the King in the Temple. He was an ardent botanist, and occupied the Chair of Botany at the *Jardin du Roi*.

accompanied by a great number of Municipal Officers: he was searched, and not permitted to speak, but in a loud voice. Once when the King had taken medicine, M. le Monnier begged to stay some hours with him: as he continued standing, while the Municipal Officers were sitting with their hats on, His Majesty asked him to take a chair, which he refused through respect, at which the Commissioners loudly murmured. The King continued ill ten days.

Soon after, the young Prince, who slept in His Majesty's chamber, and whom the Officers would not consent to have removed to the Queen's, caught a cold which was attended with fever. The Queen was the more anxious about it, as she could not obtain permission, although she used the most fervent entreaties, to be all night with her son. During the time she was allowed to be with him she attended him with the most affectionate care. The Queen afterwards caught the same disorder, and so did Madame Royale and Madame Elizabeth. M. le Monnier was suffered to continue his visits.

I fell ill in my turn. My room was damp, and without a fire-place, and the little air I breathed in it was confined by the slanting screen at the window. I was attacked with a rheumatic fever and great pain in the side that forced me to keep my bed. I got up the first morning to wait upon the King, but His Majesty, seeing the state I was in, would not suffer it, but ordered me to go to bed, and dressed the Dauphin himself.

During the first day the Dauphin scarcely ever left me; he brought me all that I drank. At night, the King took an opportunity, when he was least observed, to come into my room: he made me take a glass of cooling liquor, and said to me, with a kindness that brought tears into my eyes: 'I wish I could attend you myself, but you know how we are watched: keep up your spirits; to-morrow you will see my Physician.' At supper-time, the Royal Family came into my room, and Madame Elizabeth, unperceived by the Municipal Officer, gave me a small bottle of linctus. Though she had a violent cold, she deprived herself of the medicine to give it to me: I wished to have declined it, but she insisted upon my taking it. After supper, the Queen undressed the Prince and put him to bed, and Madame Elizabeth rolled the King's hair.

The next morning, M. le Monnier ordered me to be bled, but the consent of the Commune was necessary for the admission of a Surgeon. They talked of removing me to the Palace of the Temple; but fearing I should never be permitted to return to the Tower, if once I went out of it, I excused myself from the bleeding, and even pretended to be better. At night, we had new Municipal Officers, and nothing more was said about removing me.

Turgy asked if he might sit up with me at night, which he and his two comrades were allowed to do, and they took it in turn. I was six days confined to my bed, and the Royal Family came to see me every day. Madame Elizabeth often brought me medicines which she ordered as for herself. So many kind attentions greatly recruited my strength, and instead of feeling pain I very soon only felt gratitude and admiration.

Who would not have been affected at seeing this august Family, forgetting their own protracted miseries, to attend the sick bed of one of their servants!

Here I must not forget to relate an action of the Dauphin's, which proves how great was the goodness of his heart, and how he profited by the example of virtue which he had continually before his eyes.

One evening after putting him to bed, I withdrew to make place for the Queen and Princesses, who went to kiss him in his bed, and wish him good night. Madame Elizabeth, who had been prevented from speaking to me by the watchfulness of the Municipal Officers, took that time to put into his hand a little box of ipecacuana lozenges, desiring him to give it to me when I came back. The Queen and Princesses went up to their apartments, the King retired to his closet, and I took my supper. It was eleven o'clock before I went back to the King's chamber to turn down His Majesty's bed: I was alone, and the Prince called me in a low voice: I was much surprised to find him awake, and fearing he was ill, asked what was the matter. 'Nothing,' said he, 'only my aunt left me a little box for you, and I would not go to sleep before I gave it you; I am glad you are come, for my eyes have been already shut several times.' The tears came into mine: he perceived them, kissed me, and in two minutes was fast asleep.

To this sensibility the Prince added a great many attractions, and all the amiable qualities of his age. He would often by his *naïveté*, the liveliness of his disposition, and his little frolics, make his august parents forget their mournful situation; yet he felt it himself: he knew, young as he was, that he was in a prison, and that he was watched by enemies. His words and actions had assumed that circumspection which instinct prompts perhaps at every age under circumstances of danger. I never heard him speak either of the Tuileries, or of Versailles, or of any object that could recall to the King or Queen a painful recollection. If he saw a Municipal Officer more civil than his colleagues coming, away he ran to the Queen in haste to tell her of it, saying, with his countenance full of satisfaction: 'Mamma, it is Mr So-and-So today.'

One day, he kept his eyes fixed upon a Municipal Officer, whom he said he recollected: the man asked him where he had seen him, but the Prince refused to answer; then leaning over to the Queen: 'It was', said he to her in a low voice, 'in our journey to Varennes.'

The following anecdote affords another proof of his sensibility. There was a stone-cutter employed in making holes at the antechamber door to admit enormous bolts; the Prince, while the man was eating his breakfast, played with his tools: the King took the mallet and chisel out of his son's hands, and showed him how to handle them. He used them for some minutes. The workman, moved at seeing the King so employed, said to His Majesty: 'When you leave this Tower you will be able to say that you had worked yourself at your own prison.' 'Ah!' replied the King, 'when and how shall I leave?' The Dauphin burst into tears, and the King, letting fall the mallet and chisel, returned to his room, where he walked about hastily and in great agitation.

O N the second of December, the Municipality of the tenth of August was superseded by another, with the title of Provisional Municipality. Many of the former Municipal Officers were re-elected. I at first supposed that this new body might be of a better composition than the former, and I hoped some favourable changes in the regulation of the prison; but I was disappointed. Several of the new Officers gave me reason to regret their predecessors: they were still coarser in their manners, but I found it easy, from their way of talking, to make myself acquainted with whatever they knew. I had to study the Members of this new Municipality in order to judge of their conduct and disposition: the former ones were more insolent, the malice of the latter was more systematic and refined.

Till this period, the King had been attended only by one Municipal Officer, and the Queen by another. The new Municipality ordered that there should be two to each, and thenceforward I found it more difficult to speak with the King and the Royal Family. On the other hand, the Council, which had hitherto been held in one of the halls in the Palace of the Temple, was removed to a chamber on the ground floor of the Tower. The new Municipal Officers were desirous of surpassing the former in zeal, and this zeal was an emulation of tyranny.

On the seventh of December, an Officer at the head of a deputation of the Commune came to the King, and read a decree, ordering that the persons in confinement should be deprived of 'knives, razors, scissors, and all other sharp instruments, which are usually taken from criminals, and that the strictest search should be made for the same, as well on their persons as in their apartments'. In reading this his voice faltered: it was easy to perceive the violence he did to his feelings, and he has since shown by his conduct, that he had consented to come to the Temple, only in the hope of being useful to the Royal Family.

The King took out of his pockets a knife and a small Morocco pocket-book, from which he gave the pen-knife and scissors. The Officers searched every corner of the apartment, and carried off the razors, the curling irons, the powder-scraper, tooth-picks, and other articles of gold and silver. The same search was made in my room, and I was ordered to empty my pockets.

They then went up to the Queen, read the decree over again to her and the Princesses, and deprived them even of the little articles they used for their needlework.

An hour afterwards, I was summoned to the Council Chamber, where I was asked if I did not know what were the articles that remained in the pocket-book, which the King had returned to his pocket. 'I order you', said a Municipal Officer named Sermaize, 'to take the pocket-book away to-night.' I replied that it was not my business to put the decrees of the Commune into execution, nor to search the King's pockets. 'Cléry is in the right,' said another Municipal Officer, addressing himself to Sermaize, 'it was your business to have made the search.'

A note was made of all the articles taken from the Royal Family, which were put up in separate packets and sealed. I was then commanded to sign my name to an order, by which I was enjoined to give notice to the Council if I found any sharp instruments in possession of the King or Royal Family, or in any of their apartments. These different articles were all sent to the Commune.

By examining the registers of the Council of the Temple, it may be seen that I had often been compelled to sign decrees and demands of which I was very far from approving either the form or substance. I never did sign anything, say anything, or do anything but as specially directed by the King or Queen. A refusal on my part might have separated me from their Majesties, to whom I had devoted my existence; my signature at the bottom of certain decrees only went to show that they had been read to me.

Sermaize, the same person of whom I have been speaking, went with me to His Majesty's apartment. The King was sitting at the fire, with the tongs in his hand. Sermaize desired by authority of the Council to see what was left in the pocket-book: the King took it out of his pocket and opened it. It contained a turn-screw, tinder and a little steel. Sermaize made him give them up. The King turning on his heel, asked if the tongs he held in his hand were not also a sharp instrument? When the Municipal Officer was gone down I had an opportunity of informing His Majesty of all that had passed at the Council relative to this second search.

At dinner time, a dispute arose amongst the Commissioners. Some were against the Royal Family's

7

using knives and forks, others were for letting them have the forks, and it was at last decided that no change should be made, but that the knives and forks should be taken away after every meal.

The Queen and the Princesses were the more sensible of the loss of the little articles that had been taken from them, as they were in consequence forced to give up different works, which till then had served to divert their attention during the tedious days of a prison. Once as Madame Elizabeth was mending the King's coat, having no scissors, she bit off the thread with her teeth. 'What a contrast!' said the King, looking tenderly on her, 'you were in want of nothing at your pretty house at Montreuil.' 'Ah! brother,' replied she, 'can I feel regret of any kind when I share your misfortunes?'

Meanwhile, every day brought new decrees, every one of which was a fresh tyranny. The rude harshness of the Municipal Officers towards me was more remarkable than ever. The three attendants were again forbidden to speak to me, and every thing seemed to forebode some new misfortune. The Queen and Madame Elizabeth felt the same presentiment, and were continually applying to me for news, which it was not in my power to give. I did not expect to see my wife for three days; my impatience was extreme.

At length, on Thursday, my wife came. I was called to the Council Chamber. She affected to speak loud to avoid the suspicions of our new inspectors, and while she was giving me an account of our domestic affairs, her friend, in a lower voice, told me that on the succeeding Tuesday, the King was to be carried to the Convention, that he was to be put upon his trial, that he was to be allowed counsel: all this was certain.

I was at a loss how to announce this horrible news to the King; I wished first to inform the Queen or Madame Elizabeth of it, but I was greatly alarmed: there was no time to be lost, and the King had expressly forbidden me to conceal anything from him. At night, when I was undressing him, I told him what I had heard, and went so far as to hint that there was an intention of separating him from his Family during the trial, adding that there were but four days more to concert with the Queen some mode of corresponding with her. I also assured him that there was nothing I was not resolved to undertake to assist in it. Here the appearance of the Municipal Officers did not permit me to say more upon the subject, and prevented His Majesty from making any answer.

The next morning, I could not find an opportunity of speaking to the King when he was getting up: he went with the Dauphin to breakfast in the Queen's apartment, where I attended him. After breakfast he continued some time conversing with the Queen, who, by a look full of grief, made me understand that the intelligence I had given the King was the subject of their conversation. In the course of the day, finding an opportunity of speaking to Madame Elizabeth, I mentioned to her how much pain it had cost me to increase the sufferings of the King, by informing him of the day on which he was to be brought to trial. It was much comfort to me to hear her say that the King felt that mark of my attachment. 'What afflicts him most', added she, 'is the dread of being separated from us; endeavour to gain some further intelligence.'

That evening, the King assured me that he was very glad to have been apprised that he was to appear before the Convention. 'Continue', said he, 'to endeavour to find out what they are going to do with me, and don't be afraid of giving me pain. I have agreed with my Family not to appear informed of what is passing, that you may not be suspected.'

The nearer the day of the trial approached, the more was I distrusted: the Municipal Officers would not answer any of my questions. I had in vain been forming different pretences to go down to the Council, where I might have collected fresh particulars to communicate to the King, when a Commission arrived at the Temple, charged with auditing the accounts of the Royal Family. They were under the necessity of having me present to speak to the expenses, and I learnt through a Municipal Officer, whose dispositions were friendly, that the decree for separating the King from his Family had been passed only in the Commune, and not yet in the National Assembly. On the same day, Turgy brought me a newspaper containing the decree which ordained that the King should be brought to the bar of the Convention: he also gave me a Memorial, published by M. Necker,* on the King's trial. The only

* Jacques Necker was born in Geneva, and became a banker in Paris, where he won a reputation for honesty and integrity. He was twice Minister of Finance, and tried to introduce financial reforms. His daughter was the well-known writer, Madame de Staël.

means I had of communicating this newspaper and Memorial to the Royal Family was by hiding them under a piece of furniture in the King's water-closet. Having informed the Family of the circumstance, they had it in their power successively to read them. This closet was the only place into which the Municipal Officers did not follow them.

O N the eleventh of December 1792, by five o'clock in the morning, the drums were heard beating to arms throughout Paris, and a troop of horse with cannon were marched into the garden of the Temple. This noise would have alarmed the Royal Family, had they not been apprised of the cause: they feigned, however, to be ignorant of it, and asked an explanation of the Commissioners on duty, who refused to make any reply.

At nine o'clock, the King and the Dauphin went up to breakfast with the Queen and Princesses: their Majesties remained together an hour, but always in sight of the Municipal Officers. This constant torment which the Royal Family suffered in not being able to give loose to any unrestrained expression of their feelings, to any free effusion of their hearts, at a moment when they could not but be agitated with so many fears, was one of the most cruel refinements and dearest delights of their tyrants. They were at last obliged to part. The King left the Queen, Madame Elizabeth and his daughter, and what they dared not speak their looks expressed: the Dauphin came down as usual with the King.

The Prince, who often prevailed on His Majesty to play a game of Siam with him, was so pressing that day that the King, in spite of his situation, could not refuse him. The Dauphin lost every game, and twice he could get no farther than *sixteen*. 'Whenever', cried he in a little pet, 'I get to the point of *sixteen*, I am sure never to win the game.' The King said nothing, but he seemed to feel the coincidence of the words.

At eleven o'clock, when the King was hearing the Dauphin read, two Municipal Officers walked in and told His Majesty that they were come to carry the young Louis to his mother. The King desired to know why he was taken away: the Commissioners replied that they were executing the orders of the Council of the Commune. The King tenderly embraced his son, and charged me to conduct him. On my return I assured His Majesty that I had delivered the Prince to the Queen, which appeared to relieve his mind. One of the Municipal Officers came back and informed him that Chambon, Mayor of Paris, was with the Council, and that he was just coming up. 'What does he want with me?' said the King. The Officer answered that he did not know.

His Majesty for some minutes walked about his room in much agitation, then sat down in an arm-chair at the head of the bed: the door stood ajar, but the Officer did not like to go in, wishing, as he told me, to avoid questions. Half an hour passing thus in dead silence, he became uneasy at not hearing the King move, and went softly in: he found him leaning with his head upon his hand, apparently deep in thought.

The King, on being disturbed, said, raising his voice: 'What do you want with me?' 'I was afraid', answered the Officer, 'that you were ill.' 'I am obliged to you,' replied the King, in an accent full of anguish, 'but the manner in which they have taken my son from me cuts me to the heart.' The Municipal Officer withdrew without saying a word.

The Mayor did not make his appearance till one o'clock. He was accompanied by Chaumette, Solicitor to the Commune, Coulombeau, Secretary of the Rolls, several Municipal Officers, and Santerre, Commander in Chief of the National Guards, attended by his aides-de-camp. The Mayor told the King that he came to conduct him to the Convention, by virtue of a decree, which the Secretary to the Commune would read to him. The import of the decree was, 'that Louis Capet should be brought to the bar of the National Convention'. 'Capet', said the King, 'is not my name: it is that of one of my Ancestors.' He added, 'I could have wished, Sir, that the Commissioners had left my son with me during the two hours I have passed waiting for you: but this treatment is of a piece with the rest I have met with here for these four months. I am ready to follow you, not in obedience to the Convention, but because my enemies have the power in their hands.' I gave His Majesty his great coat and hat, and he followed the Mayor. A strong body of guards was waiting for him at the gate of the Temple.

Remaining alone in the chamber with a Municipal Officer, I learnt from him that the King was not to see his Family again, but that the Mayor had still to consult with some Deputies respecting this separation. I begged to be conducted to the Dauphin, who was with the Queen, and this was granted me. I stayed with him till about six in the evening, when the King returned from the Convention. The Municipal Officers informed the Queen of the King's departure but without entering into any particulars. The Family came down as usual to dine in His Majesty's apartment, and then went up again.

After dinner, there was but one Municipal Officer remained with the Queen. He was a young man about four-and-twenty years old, of the Section of the Temple: it was the first time he had ever been upon guard at the Tower, and he appeared less suspicious, and less uncivil than the generality of his colleagues. The Queen entered into conversation with him, and asked him questions about his situation, his family and the like. Madame Elizabeth took this opportunity of beckoning me to follow her to another room.

Here I informed her that the Commune had decreed to separate the King from his Family, and that I was afraid the separation would take place that very night: for though it was true that nothing respecting it had been done in the Convention, yet the Mayor was charged to make the application, and would no doubt succeed. 'The Queen and myself', replied she, 'look for the worst, and do not deceive ourselves as to the fate preparing for the King. He will die a sacrifice to the goodness of his heart, and love for his people, for whose happiness he has never ceased to labour since he mounted the Throne. How cruelly is this people

deceived! As for him, his Religion, and that perfect
reliance he has upon Providence, will support him in
this sad moment of adversity. You, Cléry,' continued
this virtuous Princess, with tears in her eyes, 'will now
be the only person with my brother: redouble, if
possible, your attentions to him, and omit no opportunity of giving us intelligence respecting him; but
on no other account expose yourself, for then we
should have nobody on whom we could rely.' I repeated to her my assurances of devotion to the King,
and we agreed upon means by which we could keep up
a correspondence.

Turgy was the only person I could entrust with the
secret, and to him I could speak but seldom and
cautiously. It was agreed that I should continue to
keep the Dauphin's linen and clothes; that every other
day I should send him a change, and take the opportunity to give intelligence of what was passing about
the King. This plan suggested to Madame Elizabeth
the idea of my receiving one of her handkerchiefs,
'which', said she, 'you will keep when my brother is
well, but if he should be ill, you will send it among my
nephew's linen.' The manner of folding it was to show
the nature of the disorder.

The anguish of the Princess, while speaking of her
brother, her indifference as to herself, the value which
she was pleased to attach to my poor endeavours in the
service of His Majesty, all deeply affected me. 'Have
you heard anything respecting the Queen?' said she,
with a sort of terror: 'Alas! of what can they accuse
her?' 'Nay, Madame,' I replied, 'of what can they

accuse the King?' 'Oh! nothing; no, nothing'; she answered, 'but, perhaps, they may look upon the King as a victim necessary to their safety; but surely the Queen and her children would be no obstacles to their ambition!' I took the liberty of observing that, no doubt, the King could only be sentenced to banishment, that I had heard it spoken of, and that as Spain had not declared war, it was likely that he would be sent with his Family into that kingdom. 'I have no hope', said she, 'that the King will be saved.'

I thought it proper to add that the foreign powers were busy in forming plans to extricate the King from his imprisonment; that Monsieur, and the Comte d'Artois,* were again assembling all the émigrés, to join the Austrian and Prussian armies; that Spain and England would take steps, and that all Europe was interested to prevent the death of the King; that the Convention would therefore have to reflect seriously before they pronounced upon His Majesty's fate.

This conversation lasted near an hour, when Madame Elizabeth, with whom I had never spoken for so long a time, fearing the arrival of the new Municipal Officers, left me, in order to return to the Queen's Chamber. Tison and his wife, who were perpetually watching me, observed that I had been a great while with Madame Elizabeth, and that it was to be feared the Commissioner had perceived it. I told them that

* *Monsieur* was the title given to the next younger brother of the reigning sovereign the Comte de Provence. The Comte d'Artois was Louis XVI's youngest brother, afterwards King Charles X.

the Princess had been speaking to me about her nephew, who would probably in future remain with his mother.

I returned in a few minutes to Her Majesty's chamber, to whom Madame Elizabeth had been communicating her conversation with me, and the means we had concerted for effecting a correspondence; Her Majesty had the goodness to express her satisfaction.

At six o'clock, the Commissioners took me down to the Council, where they read to me a decree of the Commune, ordering that I should no longer have any communication with the Queen, the Princesses or the young Prince, because I was appointed to wait upon the King alone. It was even decreed at first, with a view of putting the King into some sort of close confinement, that I should not sleep in his apartments, but be lodged in the little Tower, and only conducted to His Majesty when he wanted me.

At half after six o'clock, the King returned: he appeared fatigued, and the first thing he did was to desire to be taken to his Family. This was objected to, under the pretence of having no orders: he insisted that they should at least be informed of his return, which was promised him. The King then ordered me to speak for his supper at half past eight; he employed the interval of two hours in reading as usual, but all the while surrounded by four Municipal Officers.

At half past eight, I informed His Majesty that supper was served. He asked the Commissioners if his Family were not coming down: they made him no answer. 'But at least', said the King, 'my son is to sleep in my

apartment, as his bed and things are here.' Still no
reply. After supper, the King again insisted that he see
his Family: he was told that he must wait the deter-
mination of the Convention. I then delivered up the
Dauphin's night things.

When I was undressing the King for bed, he said
that he could never have conceived all the questions
they had put to him; and then lay down with great
tranquillity. The decree of the Commune, relative to
lodging me at a distance, was not put into execution: it
would have been too troublesome for the Municipal
Officers to have come for me every time the King
wanted my attendance.

On the morning of the twelfth, the moment the
King saw a Municipal Officer, he asked if there had
been any decision respecting the request he had made
to see his Family. He was again answered that they
waited for orders. He then begged that Officer to go
and enquire how the Queen, the Princesses, and the
Dauphin were, and tell them that he was well. The
Commissioner returned with an account of their being
in good health. The King then gave me orders to
send his son's bed up to the Queen's apartments,
where the young Prince had slept on one of her
mattresses. I begged His Majesty to wait the decision
of the Convention, to which he replied: 'I expect no
consideration, no justice, but let us wait.'

The same day, a deputation from the Convention,
composed of four Deputies, Thuriot, Cambacérès,*

* Jean Jacques Régis de Cambacérès was the French 'Vicar
of Bray', who always trimmed his sails to the prevailing wind.

Dubois-Crancé and Dupont de Bigorre, brought the decree authorizing the King to employ Counsel. He said, he chose M. Target, or if he declined, M. Tronchet, but both of them, if the National Convention would agree to it. The Deputies made the King sign this demand, and countersigned it themselves. His Majesty added that he should want paper, pen and ink. He gave 'M. Tronchet's address, at his country house, but said he did not know where M. Target lived.

On the thirteenth, in the morning, the same deputation returned to the Temple, and informed the King that M. Target had declined taking his defence upon him, and that M. Tronchet had been sent for, and was expected in the course of the day. They then read to him several letters which were addressed to the

---

When the Revolution broke out in 1789, Cambacérès adopted its principles. Becoming deputy to the National Convention in 1792, he voted for the King's death with conditional suspension. Tracing his steps with the utmost care, he succeeded in preserving his life when so many of his colleagues failed to do so. On the establishment of the Consulate, Cambacérès became second Consul, holding the Ministry of Justice. Under the Empire he received every possible honour, becoming Arch-Chancellor. At the Restoration he gave his vote to the Act of Senate which recalled the Bourbon dynasty. When Napoleon returned from Elba, Cambacérès was recalled to power, but did his utmost to avoid being mixed up in the uncertain political scene. The second return of Louis XVIII was the occasion of his being charged as a regicide, an accusation which was soon dropped, and in 1818 he was recalled to France from his exile in Brussels and Amsterdam, and lived more or less in retirement. He died of apoplexy in 1824.

Convention by M. Sourdat, M. Huet, M. Guillaume, and M. de Lamoignon de Malesherbes, who had been formerly first President of the Court of Aids in Paris, and afterwards Minister of the King's Household. M. de Malesherbes' letter was as follows:

Paris, December 11*th,* 1792

CITIZEN PRESIDENT,

I am yet uninformed whether the Convention will allow the defence of Louis XVI to be undertaken by Counsel or not. If it be allowed, and the choice of Counsel be left to him, I request that Louis XVI may know that, if he thinks proper to choose me for that office, I am ready to undertake it. I do not ask you to make my offer known to the Convention, for I am far from thinking myself of sufficient importance to engage their attention, but I was twice appointed a Member of the Council of him who was my Master, at a time when that office excited a general ambition: I feel it to be my duty to offer myself as his Counsel now that that duty is thought dangerous by many. If I knew any possible mode of making my intention known to him, I should not take the liberty of applying to you. I imagine the place you fill affords you the means, more than any other person, of sending him this information.

I am, with respect, &c.

L. DE MALESHERBES

His Majesty said, 'I receive with sensibility the offers of the gentlemen who desire to be my Counsel, and

I request you to express my acknowledgments to them. I accept that of M. de Malesherbes. If I cannot have M. Tronchet's services, I shall consult M. de Malesherbes on the choice of another.'

O N the fourteenth of December, M. Tronchet had a conference with His Majesty, agreeably to the decree. On the same day, M. de Malesherbes was introduced into the Tower. The King ran to meet this venerable man, and pressed him affectionately to his bosom, while the old statesman melted into tears at the sight of his Master— whether it was that the first happy years of that Master's reign rushed upon his memory, or rather that he saw at that moment only the virtuous man struggling with adversity. As the King had permission to consult with his Counsel in private, I shut his chamber door that he might be able to speak more freely with M. de Malesherbes. For this I was reprimanded by a Municipal Officer, who ordered me to open it, and forbade my shutting it in future; I opened the door, but His Majesty had withdrawn to the turret-closet.

In this first conference, the King and M. de Malesherbes spoke very loud: the Commissioners, who were in the chamber, listened to their conversation, and could hear everything. When M. de Malesherbes was gone, I informed His Majesty of the prohibition I had received from them, and of the attention with which they had listened to the conference, begging that he would himself shut the door of his chamber when his Counsel were with him, which, in future, he did.

On the fifteenth, the King received an answer relative to his Family, which was in substance, that the Queen and Madame Elizabeth should have no communication with the King during the trial, but that his children might be with him, if he desired it, on condition that they were not allowed to see their mother or their aunt, till his examination was concluded. The first moment I could speak to His Majesty in private, I asked for his orders. 'You see', said the King, 'the cruel dilemma in which they have placed me. I cannot think of having my children with me: as for my daughter, she is out of the question, and I know what pain the Queen would suffer in giving up my son: I must make the sacrifice.' His Majesty then repeated his orders for the removal of the Prince's bed, which I immediately executed. I kept his linen and clothes, and sent him a change every other day, as had been agreed upon with Madame Elizabeth.

On the sixteenth, at four in the afternoon, there came another deputation of four Members of the Convention: Valazé,* Cochon, Grandpré, and Duprat,

* Charles Éléonore du Friche de Valazé, in early life a regular soldier, later became a farmer. He then turned to writing, his book on the *Lois pénales* gaining him considerable appreciation. In 1792 he was elected Deputy for the Department of the Orne, and attacked Marat in the Assembly. During the King's trial he spoke at length in an endeavour to prove Louis' guilt in conspiring with the enemies of France. Valazé made up for much by his courageous resistance to Robespierre, protesting

part of the Committee of Twenty-one, appointed to superintend the King's trial. They were accompanied by a Secretary, a tipstaff, and an Officer of the Guard belonging to the Convention: they brought the King a copy of his impeachment, and papers relative to the proceedings against him, the greater part of which were found at the Tuileries in a secret press in His Majesty's apartments, called by the Minister Roland,* the Iron Press.†

The reading of these papers, to the number of one hundred and seven, lasted from four o'clock till

---

energetically against his tyranny and cruelty. He was in consequence arrested and condemned to death. On hearing the sentence he stabbed himself secretly with a dagger he had hidden in his clothing, and when the man next him gibed at him, saying, 'You are trembling, Valazé', he replied, 'No, I am dying', and fell dead. His corpse was carried to the scaffold, where the rest of the Girondins met the same fate.

* Jean Marie Roland de la Platière was Minister of the Interior. His chief claim to fame is that he was his wife's husband. He was a moderate, of the party of the Gironde. After his wife's execution (it will be remembered that it was she who on this occasion uttered the famous words, 'Liberty! What crimes are committed in thy name!') he wrote a farewell letter to the person who should find his body, and sitting under a tree, stabbed himself with his sword-stick, like the Romans whom he so greatly admired.

† The 'Iron Press' was a safe in the Tuileries palace, whose lock, according to tradition, was made by Louis XVI, who had a keen interest in the work of a locksmith and spent many happy hours dabbling in the craft. It was believed to have contained compromising papers which proved the King guilty of conspiring with enemy powers.

midnight. They were all read and marked by the King, as likewise copies of them, which were left in his hands. The King sat at a large table, with M. Tronchet by his side; the Deputies sat opposite to him. After the reading of each piece, Valazé asked the King if he had any knowledge of it, and similar questions. His Majesty answered yes or no, without further explanation. A second Deputy gave him the papers and copies to sign, and a third offered to read them over again each time, with which His Majesty always dispensed. It was the business of the fourth to call over the papers by packets and by numbers, and the Secretary entered them on a register one by one as they were handed to the King.

His Majesty interrupted the sitting to ask the Deputies of the Convention if they would not go to supper; to this they consented, and I served a cold fowl and some fruit in the eating-room. M. Tronchet would not take anything, and remained alone with the King in his chamber.

A Municipal Officer, named Merceraut, at that time a stone-cutter, and late President of the Commune of Paris, though a chairman at Versailles before the Revolution, happened to be upon guard at the Temple for the first time. He had on his working clothes, which were in rags, an old worn-out round hat, a leather apron, and his tricolor scarf. This fellow had the affectation to stretch himself out by the King in an arm-chair, while His Majesty was sitting on a common chair, and with his hat on his head, *thee'd* and *thou'd* everybody who addressed any conversation to him: the Members of the Convention were astonished at it, and one of them, during supper, asked me several questions concerning this Merceraut, and of the manner in which the Municipality treated the King. To this I was going to answer when another Commissioner told him to discontinue his questions, that it was forbidden to speak with me, and that in the Council Chamber he should be made acquainted with every particular he could desire. The Deputy, apprehensive of having gone too far, made no reply.

The examination was now resumed. In the number of papers presented to His Majesty he took notice of the declaration which he had made on his return from Varennes, when Messrs Tronchet, Barnave* and Duport were appointed by the Constituent Assembly to receive it. This Declaration had been signed by the King and the Deputies. 'You will admit the authenticity of this paper,' said the King to M. Tronchet, 'your own signature is to it.'

Some of the packets contained plans for a Constitution, with marginal notes written in His Majesty's

---

* Antoine Pierre Joseph Marie Barnave was one of the three members of the Assembly sent to bring the King back to Paris after his arrest at Varennes. At the Assembly he fought hard to ensure the inviolability of the King's person, but to no avail. He consequently retired to his birthplace, Grenoble, married, and left political life. Certain compromising letters between a member of the Court and some members of the Assembly were, however, found at the Tuileries; Barnave was involved, and he was arrested and imprisoned. After spending more than a year in prison at Grenoble, he was brought to Paris, where he was condemned to death by the Revolutionary Tribunal, and guillotined on October 29, 1793, at the age of thirty-two.

hand; several of these were in ink, and several in pencil. Some registers of the Police were also shown to the King, in which there were informations written and signed by his own servants: His Majesty seemed much affected by this proof of ingratitude. These informers pretended to relate occurrences that passed in the King's or Queen's apartments in the Palace of the Tuileries only to give more appearance of probability to their calumnies.

After the Members of the Deputation had retired, the King took some refreshment, and went to bed without complaining of the fatigue he had suffered. He only asked me if his Family had been kept waiting for supper: on my replying in the negative 'I should have been afraid', said he, 'that the delay would have made them uneasy.' He even had the goodness to find fault with me for not supping before him.

Some days after, the four members of the Committee of Twenty-one came again to the Temple. They read fifty-one new papers to the King, which he signed and marked as he had done the former, making in the whole 158 papers of which copies were left with him.

From the fourteenth to the twenty-sixth of December, the King regularly saw his Counsel, who came at five in the afternoon and returned at nine. M. de Sèze was added to the number. Every morning M. de Malesherbes brought His Majesty the newspapers, and printed opinions of the Deputies respecting his trial. He arranged the business for every evening, and stayed an hour or two with His Majesty. The King often had

The King gives the Dauphin a Geography Lesson

the condescension to give me some of the printed opinions to read, and would afterwards ask me what I thought of the opinion of such a one. I told His Majesty I wanted words to express my indignation; 'but you, Sire,' said I, 'I wonder how you can read it all without horror.' 'I see the extent of men's wickedness,' replied the King, 'and I did not believe that such could exist.' His Majesty never went to bed till he had read these different papers, and then, in order not to involve M. de Malesherbes, he took care to burn them himself, at the stove in his closet.

I had by this time found a favourable opportunity of speaking to Turgy, and of charging him with news of the King to Madame Elizabeth. Turgy apprised me next morning, that, in giving him her napkin after dinner, she had slipped into his hand a little piece of paper, on which she had punctured with a pin her desire that I should beg the King to write her a line with his own hand. This I communicated to His Majesty that same evening. As he had been furnished with paper and ink since the beginning of his trial, he wrote his Sister a note, which he gave me unsealed, saying that it contained nothing that could endanger me, and desired me to read it. In this last particular, I besought His Majesty to allow me for the first time to disobey him.

The next day I gave the note to Turgy, who brought an answer in a ball of cotton, which he threw under my bed as he passed my chamber door. His Majesty saw with great pleasure that this mode of hearing from his Family had succeeded, and I observed

to him that it was easy to continue the correspondence.
On receiving notes from His Majesty, I folded them
into as small a size as I could, and wound cotton about
them; I then put them into the cupboard where the
plates were kept for dinner; Turgy found them there,
and made use of different means to return me the
answers. When I gave them to the King, he always
said with kindness to me: 'Take care; you expose
yourself too much.'

The wax tapers, which the Commissioners sent me,
were tied up in packages. When I had collected a
sufficient quantity of the packthread, I observed to the
King that it now depended on himself to carry on the
correspondence with more dispatch, by conveying
some of this packthread to Madame Elizabeth, whose
room was over mine, and the window of which was in
a direct line above that of a small corridor to which
my chamber opened. The Princess, in the night, could
tie her letters to this packthread, and let them down to
the window that was under hers. A sort of screen,
something resembling a scuttle, at each window, prevented the possibility of her letters falling into the
garden; and, by the same means, the Princess might
receive answers. A little paper and ink, of which the
Queen and Princesses had been deprived, might also
be tied to the packthread. 'The project is a good one',
said His Majesty, 'and we will make use of it, if that
which we have hitherto employed should become
impracticable.' It was actually practised in the sequel
by the King. He used always to wait till eight o'clock
at night for the purpose; I then shut the doors of my

chamber and the corridor, and talked with the Commissioners, or engaged them at play, to divert their attention.

It was about this time that Marchand, one of the servants in attendance, who was father of a family and had just received his wages for two months amounting to 200 livres, was robbed in the Temple. The loss to him was serious. The King, who had observed his dejection, being informed of the cause, desired me to give him the 200 livres, and to charge him at the same time not to mention it to anybody, and particularly not to attempt to thank him; 'for', added the King, 'that would be his destruction'. Marchand was sensibly touched by His Majesty's bounty, but still more so by the prohibition to express his gratitude.

Since his separation from the Royal Family, the King had constantly refused to go down to the garden. When it was proposed to him, his reply was: 'I cannot think of going out by myself; I only found the walk agreeable by enjoying it with my Family.' But, though deprived of the dearest objects of his heart, and certain of the destiny that awaited himself, he suffered not a complaint, nor a murmur, to escape his lips. He had already forgiven his oppressors. Every day, in his reading-closet, he acquired new strength to sustain his natural fortitude; those hours which he passed out of it were spent in the details of a life always uniform, but always adorned with numberless instances of goodness. He condescended to treat me as if I had been more than his servant. He behaved to the Municipal Officers who guarded him as if he had no reason to complain of them, and talked with them, as he used formerly to do with any of his subjects, about their occupations, their families, the advantages, and the duties of their respective situations. They were astonished at the justness of his remarks, at the variety of his ideas, and at the method with which they were classed in his memory. His object, in these conversations, was not to divert his mind from the recollection of his sufferings; his sensibility was both active and strong, but his resignation was still superior to his misfortunes.

On the nineteenth of December, breakfast was brought as usual for the King; it was Wednesday, but not thinking of the Ember Weeks, I presented it to him. 'This is a fast-day', said he, and I carried the breakfast back to the eating-room. The Municipal Officer (one Dorat de Cubières) said deridingly to me: 'No doubt you will follow your master's example, and fast too.' 'No, Sir,' I replied, 'I have need of some breakfast to-day.' Some days after, His Majesty gave me a newspaper to read, which had been brought by M. de Malesherbes, where I found this anecdote entirely misrepresented. 'There,' said the King, 'you will see that they have given you the character of a mischief maker; they would much rather have given you that of an hypocrite.'

The same day, the nineteenth, at dinner, the King said to me before three or four Municipal Officers: 'This day fourteen years ago you were up earlier than you were this morning.' I immediately understood His Majesty, who added: 'My daughter was born that day.' He then exclaimed with emotion: 'And I am not to see her on her birthday!' Some tears trickled down his cheeks, and for a moment there was a respectful silence.

The King sent word to Madame Royale that he wished to know what present she chose he should make her. She desired to have an almanack like the little Court Calendar, which the King ordered me to get, and also the Republican Almanack for him, which had superseded the Royal Almanack. He often looked it over, and marked the names with a pencil.

The King was now soon to make his appearance at the bar of the Convention. He had not been shaved since his razors had been taken away, and his beard had been very troublesome to him. He was obliged to bathe his face in cold water several times every day. He desired me to procure for myself a pair of scissors, or a razor, for he did not choose to speak about it himself to the Municipal Officers. I took the liberty of suggesting that, if he would appear as he was at the Assembly, the people would at least see with what barbarity the Council General had acted towards him. 'It does not become me', said the King, 'to take steps to excite commiseration.' I applied to the Municipal Officers, and next day the Commune resolved that His Majesty's razors should be returned, but that he was not to have the liberty of using them except in the presence of two of the Officers.

For three days before Christmas, the King was more engaged than usual in writing. At this time, a design was formed of detaining him at the Feuillants for a day or two, that they might pass sentence without adjourning. I had even received orders to be ready to attend him, and to collect what he might want; but the design was given up. On Christmas day His Majesty wrote his Will. I read, and copied it, at the time when it was sent to the Council at the Temple; it was entirely written by the King's own hand, with a few erasures. I think it my duty here to set down this monument of his innocence and of his piety, now registered in Heaven.

THE WILL OF LOUIS XVI

'In the name of the Holy Trinity, of the Father, of the Son, and of the Holy Ghost; on the twenty-fifth day of December 1792, I, Louis XVI, King of France, having been more than four months immured with my Family in the Tower of the Temple at Paris, by those who were my subjects, and deprived of all communication whatsoever, even with my Family, since the eleventh of this month; involved moreover in a trial, the issue of which, from the passions of men, it is impossible to foresee, and for which there is neither pretence nor foundation in any existing law; having God only for the witness of my thoughts, and to whom I can address myself, do hereby declare, in His Presence, my last will, and the feelings of my heart.

'I render my soul to God, its Creator, beseeching him to receive it in his mercy, and not to judge it according to its own merits, but according to the merits of our Lord Jesus Christ, who offered himself a sacrifice to God his Father, for us men, unworthy of it as we were, and I above all others.

'I die in the union of our Holy Mother, the Catholic, Apostolic, and Roman Church, which holds its powers by an uninterrupted succession from St Peter, to whom they were confided by Jesus Christ.

'I firmly believe, and acknowledge all that is contained in the Creed and the Commandments, of God and of the Church, the Sacraments and Mysteries, such as the Catholic Church teaches, and has ever taught them. I have never pretended to render myself a judge in the different modes of explaining the dogmas that divide the Church of Christ, but I have ever conformed, and ever will conform, if God grant me life, to the decisions which the superior Ecclesiastics of the Holy Catholic Church have made, and shall make, according to the discipline of the Church adopted from the time of Jesus Christ.

'I grieve with all my heart for such of our brethren as may be in error: but I presume not to judge them, and do not the less love them all in Christ Jesus, as we are taught to do by Christian charity. I pray God to forgive me all my sins; I have endeavoured scrupulously to discover them, to detest them, and to humble myself in his presence. Not having it in my power to avail myself of the ministry of a Catholic Priest, I pray to God to receive the confession I have made of them to him, and especially my deep repentance for having put my name (though against my will) to instruments that may be contrary to the discipline and belief of the Catholic Church, to which I have always remained from my heart sincerely attached. I pray to God to accept my firm resolution of taking the earliest opportunity, if he grant me life, to avail myself of the ministry of a Catholic Priest, to confess all my sins and receive the Sacrament of Penance.

'I entreat all whom I may have offended through inadvertence (for I do not recollect having ever willingly given offence to any person), or to whom I may have given any bad example or scandal by my actions, to forgive the evil I may have done them. I entreat all charitable persons to unite their prayers with mine, that I may obtain pardon of God for my sins.

'I forgive with all my heart those who have become my enemies without my having given them any reasons for so doing, and I pray God to forgive them, as well as those who, through a false or misconceived zeal, have done me much evil.

'I recommend to God, my wife and my children, my sister and my aunts, my brothers, and all who are related to me by ties of blood, or in any other manner whatsoever: I pray God more especially to look with mercy upon my wife, my children, and my sister, who have been suffering a long time with me, to support them by his grace, if they lose me, and as long as they remain in this perishable world.

'I recommend my children to my wife: I have never doubted her maternal tenderness. I particularly recommend it to her to make them good Christians, and to give them virtuous minds, to make them look upon the pomps of this world, if they are condemned to experience them, as a dangerous and transitory inheritance, and to turn their thoughts to the only solid and durable glory of eternity. I entreat my sister to continue her tenderness to my children, and to be a mother to them should they have the misfortune to lose their own.

'I entreat my wife to forgive me all the evils she suffers on my account, and whatever vexations I may have caused her in the course of our union; as she may be assured that I harbour nothing against her, should she suppose there was anything with which she might reproach herself.

'I recommend most earnestly to my children, after their duty to God, which must always stand first, to continue united together, submissive and obedient to their mother, and grateful for all the cares and pains she takes for them, and in memory of me. I entreat them to look upon their aunt as a second mother.

'I recommend to my son, if he should have the misfortune of becoming King, to reflect, that he ought to devote himself entirely to the happiness of his fellow citizens; that he ought to forget all hatred and resentment, and particularly in what relates to the misfortunes and vexations I have suffered; that he cannot promote the happiness of a nation but by reigning according to the laws; yet, at the same time, that a King cannot enforce those laws, and do the good which his heart prompts, unless he be possessed of the necessary authority, for that otherwise, being fettered in his operations, and inspiring no respect, he is more hurtful than useful.

'I recommend to my son to take care of all who were attached to me, as far as circumstances may put it in his power: to recollect that it is a sacred debt which I have contracted with the children or relations of those who have perished for me, and, lastly, of those who are themselves unfortunate on my account.

'I know that there are several persons, formerly in my service, who have not conducted themselves towards me as they ought, and even shown ingratitude towards me; but I forgive them (in times of tumult and effervescence we are not always masters of ourselves), and I entreat my son, if he should ever have an opportunity, that he will think only of their misfortunes.

'I wish I could here express my acknowledgements to those who have evinced a true and disinterested attachment for me: on the one hand, if I have been keenly wounded by the ingratitude and disloyalty of people who have experienced from me nothing but bounty, either themselves or in the persons of their relations or friends; on the other hand, I have had the consolation of seeing an attachment and concern manifested for me by many on whom I never bestowed a favour: I entreat them to accept my best thanks. In the situation in which things still remain, I should be afraid of endangering them if I were more explicit; but I recommend it particularly to my son to seek occasions of showing his acknowledgment.

'I think, however, that I should do injustice to the sentiments of the nation if I hesitated openly to recommend to my son M. de Chamilly and M. Huë, whose sincere attachment to me prompted them to shut themselves up with me in this melancholy habitation, and who looked to become the unhappy victims of that attachment. I also recommend Cléry to him, with whose services ever since he has been with me I have had every reason to be entirely satisfied. As it is he who has remained with me to the last, I entreat the Gentlemen of the Commune, to see that my clothes, books, watch, purse, and the other small articles that were lodged with the Council of the Commune, be delivered to him.

'I also most freely forgive those who were guards over me, for the ill-treatment and constraint they thought it their duty to inflict upon me. Some there were whose souls were tender and compassionate; may their hearts enjoy that peace which should be the reward of such dispositions.

'I request M. de Malesherbes, M. Tronchet, and M. de Sèze, to receive here my best thanks for, and acknowledgments of, the sense I entertain of all the care and trouble they have taken upon themselves for me.

'I conclude by declaring before God, in whose presence I am about to appear, that my conscience does not reproach me with any of the crimes which are imputed to me.

'Written and signed by me, and a duplicate hereof made, at the Tower of the Temple, on the twenty-fifth day of December 1792.   LOUIS'

9

ON the twenty-sixth of December, the King was conducted the second time to the bar of the Assembly: I had taken care to have the Queen apprised of it, that she might not be alarmed by the drums, and the movements of the troops. His Majesty set out at ten o'clock in the morning, and returned at five in the evening, still in the custody of Chambon and Santerre. In the evening, just as the King got up from supper, M. de Malesherbes, M. de Sèze, and M. Tronchet, arrived: he requested them to take some refreshment, which was accepted only by M. de Sèze. To him His Majesty expressed his acknowledgments for the trouble he had taken in his speech of that day: the Gentlemen then withdrew to the cabinet.

The next day, His Majesty condescended to give me his defence, which had been printed, after asking the Municipal Officers if he might do it without impropriety. The Commissioner, Vincent, a builder, who had rendered every service in his power to the Royal Family, undertook to convey a copy of it secretly to the Queen. When the King was thanking him for executing this little commission, he availed himself of the opportunity to ask His Majesty for something which he might keep as having belonged to him. The King untied his cravat, and made him a present of it. Another time he gave his gloves to one who asked them from the same motive. Even in the eyes of many who guarded him, these spoils had already become sacred.

On the first of January, I went to the King's bedside, and in a low voice begged his permission to present him with my most ardent wishes for the termination of his misfortunes. 'I accept your good wishes,' said he, in an affectionate manner, giving me one of his hands, which I kissed and bathed with my tears. As soon as he was up, he requested a Municipal Officer to go and ask how his Family were, and to present them with his best wishes for the New Year. The Municipal Officers were softened at the manner in which these affecting words, as they referred to the situation of the King, were spoken. 'Why', said one of them to me, when His Majesty had returned to his chamber, 'does not he ask to see his Family? Now that the proceedings are gone through, there could be no difficulty in the way: but he must apply to the Convention.' The Municipal Officer who had gone with the message to the Queen's apartments, now returned, and informed His Majesty that his Family thanked him for his good wishes, and sent him theirs. 'What a New-Year's Day!' said the King.

The same evening, I took the liberty of remarking to him that I was almost sure of the consent of the Convention, if His Majesty would ask to be allowed to see his Family. 'In a few days', said the King, 'they will not refuse me that consolation: I must wait.'

The nearer the hour of pronouncing judgment approached, if the proceeding against the King can be so called, the more were my fears and anguish increased: I put a thousand questions to the Municipal Officers, and all their answers added to my terrors. My wife still came every week to see me, and gave me an exact account of what was passing in Paris. Public

opinion appeared always favourable to the King and
even burst out loudly at the theatres Français and
Vaudeville. When a play called *l'Ami des Lois* was
performed at the first of these, every allusion to His
Majesty's trial was caught and received with the most
unbounded applause. At the latter, one of the characters in *la Chaste Suzanne*, says to the two old men:
'How can you be accusers and judges at the same
time?' The audience forced the player to repeat this
passage several times over. I gave the King a copy of
l'Ami des Lois. I often told him, and indeed had almost
persuaded myself, that the Members of the Convention, divided against one another, would only sentence
him to confinement or banishment. 'May they', replied His Majesty, 'act with that moderation to my
Family! I have no fear but for them.'

Some persons gave me to understand, by means of
my wife, that a considerable sum, lodged with M.
Parisot, editor of the *Feuille du Jour*, was at the King's
disposal, concerning which I was desired to apply to
him for orders, and that the sum should be paid into
the hands of M. de Malesherbes, if agreeable to His
Majesty. I gave the King an account of it. 'Thank
those persons in my name,' replied he, 'I cannot accept
their generous offers, it would endanger them.'
I begged him at least to speak of it to M. de Malesherbes,
which he promised me to do.

The correspondence between their Majesties was
still kept up. The King being informed that Madame
Royale was ill, was very uneasy for some days, till
the Queen, after much entreaty, obtained the atten-

dance of M. Brunier, Physician to the Children of France, on which his mind seemed to be relieved.

On Tuesday, the fifteenth of January, the day before the King was to receive judgment, his Counsel came to him as usual: when M. de Sèze and M. Tronchet apprised His Majesty of their absence the next day.

On Wednesday morning, the sixteenth, M. de Malesherbes stayed a considerable time with the King, and told His Majesty as he went away that he would come and give him an account of the votes as soon as he knew the result of them; but the sitting being prolonged at night to a very late hour, the decree was not pronounced till the morning of the seventeenth.

On the evening of the sixteenth, at six o'clock, four Municipal Officers entered the room and read a decree of the Commune to the King, importing in substance 'that he should be kept in sight, night and day, by the said four Municipal Officers, and that two of them should stay all night by his bed-side'. The King asked if the judgment had been pronounced: one of them (du Roure) having first seated himself in the arm-chair that belonged to His Majesty, who was standing, answered that he did not trouble himself about what was passing at the Convention, but he had heard say that they were still voting. A few moments after, M. de Malesherbes came in, and informed the King that the votes were not all yet taken.

At this time, the chimney of a chamber, where the wood-carrier* of the Temple Palace lodged, took fire.

* Fires in France are generally made with wood. [*Note to original English edition.*]

A considerable crowd got into the Court. A Municipal Officer in great alarm ran in to desire M. de Malesherbes to retire immediately; he went away after assuring the King that he would return to let him know the judgment. I then asked the Municipal Officer what it was that frightened him? 'The Temple is set on fire,' said he; 'it has been done on purpose to save Capet in the tumult; but I have had the walls surrounded by a strong guard.' We soon heard that the fire was extinguished, and that it had arisen from a mere accident.

On Thursday, January the seventeenth, M. de Malesherbes came about nine o'clock in the morning: I ran to meet him. 'All is lost,' said he, 'the King is condemned.' The King, who saw him coming, rose to receive him. The Minister threw himself at his feet; his voice was stifled with sobs, and, for several moments, he could not utter a word. The King raised him, and pressed him to his bosom with warmth. M. de Malesherbes then made known to him the decree sentencing him to death. The King showed no mark of surprise or agitation: he seemed affected only at the grief of that venerable old man, and even endeavoured to console him.

M. de Malesherbes gave His Majesty an account of the result of the votes. Informers, relations, personal enemies, laity, clergy, absent members, had indiscriminately given their suffrages; yet, notwithstanding this violation of all forms, those who were for death, some as a political necessity, others pretending to believe the King really guilty, amounted to a majority

The King bids farewell to his family

of *five only*. Several members had voted for the death sentence to be suspended conditionally. A second vote upon this question had been resolved; and it was to be presumed that the voices of those who were for postponing the perpetration of the regicide, joined to the suffrages against the sentence being capital, would have formed the majority. But at the gates of the Assembly, assassins, devoted to the Duke of Orleans, and to the Deputies of Paris, by their cries terrified, and with their poignards menaced whoever should refuse to become their accomplice; and thus, whether from stupefaction or indifference, the capital did not dare, or did not choose, to make a single attempt to save its King.

M. de Malesherbes was preparing to go: the King desired, and was permitted, to speak with him in private. He took him to his closet, shut the door, and remained about an hour alone with him. His Majesty then conducted him to the outer door, desired he would return early in the evening, and not forsake him in his last moments. 'The grief of this good old man has deeply affected me', said the King to me as he came back to his chamber where I was waiting for him.

From the arrival of M. de Malesherbes I had been seized with a trembling through my whole frame: however, I got everything ready for the King to shave. He put on the soap himself, standing up and facing me while I held his basin. Forced to stifle my feelings, I had not yet had resolution to look at the face of my unfortunate Master; but my eyes now catching his accidentally, my tears ran over in spite of me.

I know not whether seeing me in that state put the King in mind of his own situation or not, but he suddenly turned very pale. At this sight, my knees trembled and my strength forsook me; the King, perceiving me ready to fall, caught me by both hands, and pressing them warmly, said, in a gentle voice, 'Come, more courage.' He was observed; the depth of my affliction was manifested by my silence, of which he seemed sensible. His countenance was reanimated, he shaved himself with composure, and I then dressed him.

HIS Majesty remained in his chamber till dinner-time, employed in reading or walking. In the evening, seeing him go towards his closet, I followed him, under pretence that he might want my attendance. 'You have heard', said the King to me, 'the account of the sentence pronounced against me?' 'Ah! Sire,' I answered, 'let us hope that it will be suspended; M. de Malesherbes believes that it will.' 'I seek no hope,' replied the King, 'but I grieve exceedingly to think that Monsieur d'Orléans, my relation, should have voted for my death: read that list.' He then gave me the list of voters, which he had in his hand. 'The public', I observed, 'murmurs greatly: Dumouriez is in Paris; it is said that he entertains favourable intentions, and that he brings with him the sentiments of his army against your Majesty's trial. The people are shocked at the infamous conduct of Monsieur d'Orléans. It is also reported that the foreign Ambassadors will meet and go to the Assembly.

Indeed, it is confidently asserted, that the Members of the Convention are afraid of a popular insurrection.' 'I should be very sorry to have it take place,' replied the King, 'for then there would be new victims. I do not fear death,' added His Majesty, 'but I cannot, without shuddering, contemplate the cruel fate which I leave behind me, to my Family, to the Queen, to our unfortunate children. And those faithful servants, who have never abandoned me, and those old men, whose subsistence depended upon the little pensions I allowed them, who will succour and protect them? I see the people delivered over a prey to anarchy, to become the victims of every faction, crimes succeed crimes, long dissensions tear France in pieces.' Then, after a moment's pause: 'Oh! my God!' he exclaimed, 'is this the reward which I must receive for all my sacrifices? Have I not tried everything to ensure the happiness of the French people?' In pronouncing these words, he seized and pressed both my hands: I bathed his with my tears, and in that state I had to leave him. The King expected M. de Malesherbes, but in vain. At night he asked me if he had been at the Temple: I had put the same question to the Commissioners, who had all answered no.

On Friday, the eighteenth, the King was exceedingly uneasy at hearing no news of M. de Malesherbes. He happened to take up an old *Mercure de France*, where he found a riddle* which he gave me to guess; but not

* *Logogriphe*; a particular sort of riddle, where the word meant is described by the different words and names which may be made out of some or all the letters. (*Note to original edition.*)

being able to do it—'What, can't you find it out?' said
he, 'and yet it is at this moment very applicable to me:
Sacrifice is the word.' He then ordered me to look in
the library for the volume of Hume's *History of
England* that contained the death of Charles I, which
he read the following days. I found, on this occasion,
that His Majesty had perused, since his coming to the
Temple, two hundred and fifty volumes. At night, I
took the liberty of observing to him that he could not
be deprived of his Counsel without a decree of the
Convention, and that he might demand their admission
to the Tower. 'Let us wait till tomorrow', was his
reply.

On Saturday the nineteenth, at nine in the morning,
a Municipal Officer named Gobeau came in, holding
a paper in his hand: he was accompanied by the
Warden of the Tower, one Mathey, who brought an
inkstand. The Municipal Officer told the King that he
had orders to take an inventory of the furniture and
other effects. His Majesty left me with him, and
retired to the turret. The Municipal Officer then, under
pretence of taking the inventory, began a very minute
search, to be certain, as he said, that no arms or sharp
instruments had been secreted in His Majesty's
chamber. A small desk remained to be examined,
which contained papers: the King was compelled to
open every drawer in it, and to remove and show every
paper, one after the other. There were three rouleaux
at the bottom of one of the drawers, the contents of
which they desired to see. 'It is', said the King,
'money which does not belong to me, but to M. de

Malesherbes: I had put it up for the purpose of giving it to him.' The three rouleaux contained three thousand livres in gold; on each was written, in the King's hand, *for M. de Malesherbes.*

While the same search was being made in the turret, His Majesty went into his chamber, and wanted to warm himself. Mathey, the Warden, was standing before the fire, with his back to it, and his coat-flaps tucked up under his arms. As he scarcely left room on either side for the King to warm himself, and continued insolently standing in the same place, His Majesty, with some quickness, told him to leave a little more room. Mathey withdrew, and soon after the Municipal Officers left also, having concluded their search.

In the evening the King desired the Municipal Officers to enquire of the Commune upon what grounds they objected to his Counsel's coming to the Tower, requesting to have at least some conversation with M. de Malesherbes. They promised to mention it, but one of them confessed that they had been forbidden to lay before the Council General any application from Louis XVI unless this were written and signed by himself. 'Why', replied the King, 'have I been left two whole days ignorant of this alteration?' He then wrote a note, and gave it to the Municipal Officers, who, however, did not carry it to the Commune till the next morning. The King desired to have free communication with his Counsel, and complained of the resolution ordering him to be kept in sight both night and day. 'It must be supposed', said he, in his note to the Commune, 'that, in the situation I now am, it is very painful for me not to have it in my power to be alone, and not to be allowed the tranquillity necessary to collect myself.'

On Sunday, the twentieth of January, the King, the moment he was up, enquired of the Municipal Officers if they had laid his request before the Council of the Commune, which they assured him they had done immediately. About ten o'clock, on my going into the King's chamber, he said: 'I do not see that M. de Malesherbes comes.' 'Sir,' said I, 'I have just learnt that he came several times, but was always refused admission into the Tower.' 'I shall soon know the grounds of this refusal,' replied the King, 'as the Commune have, no doubt before this time, considered my letter.' He employed himself the rest of the morning in walking about his chamber, and in reading and writing.

Just as the clock had struck two, the door was suddenly thrown open, for the Executive Council. About a dozen or fifteen persons came forward at once. Garat, the Minister of Justice, le Brun, Minister for Foreign Affairs, Grouvelle,* Secretary to the Council, the President, and the Procurator-General-Syndic of

* Philippe Antoine Grouvelle was a writer, whose opera *Prunes*, which he wrote in collaboration with his friend Després, was twice performed before Marie Antoinette in the *petits appartements* at Versailles. On the outbreak of the Revolution he adopted its principles, and in August 1792 became Secretary of the Provisional Executive Council. He later became French Ambassador to Denmark, was recalled in 1794, and reappointed two years later.

the Department, the Mayor, and Solicitor to the Commune, the President and Public Prosecutor of the Criminal Tribunal. Santerre, stepping before the others, told me to announce the Executive Council. The King, who had heard the noise they made in coming in, had got up, and advanced some steps, but at sight of this train he stopped between his chamber door and that of the antechamber in a most noble and commanding attitude. I was close by him. Garat, with his hat upon his head, addressed him thus: 'Louis, the National Convention has charged the Provisional Executive Council to make known to you its decrees of the 15th, 16th, 17th, 19th and 20th of January. The Secretary of the Council will read them to you.' On which Grouvelle, the Secretary, unrolled the decrees, and read them with a weak and tremulous voice.

Decrees of the National Convention of the 15th, 16th, 17th, 19th and 20th of January

ARTICLE I

The National Convention declares Louis Capet, the last King of the French, guilty of a conspiracy against the liberty of the Nation, and of an attempt against the general safety of the State.

ARTICLE II

The National Convention decrees that Louis Capet shall suffer the punishment of death.

ARTICLE III

The National Convention declares null and void the instrument of Louis Capet, brought to the Bar by his

Counsel, entitled, 'An Appeal to the Nation against the Judgment passed upon him by the Convention'; and prohibits everyone whomsoever to pay any attention to it, on pain of being prosecuted and punished as guilty of an attempt against the general safety of the Republic.

ARTICLE IV

The Provisional Executive Council shall give notice of the present decree in the course of the day to Louis Capet, and shall take proper measures to carry the same into execution within twenty-four hours after such notice given, and shall give a full account thereof to the National Convention immediately after it is executed.

While this was being read, no alteration took place in the King's countenance. I observed only in the first article, at the word *conspiracy*, a smile of indignation appear upon his lips; but at the words *shall suffer the punishment of death*, the calm expression of his face, when he looked on those around him, showed them that death had no terrors for innocence. The King stepped forward, and took the decree from the hands of the Secretary Grouvelle, folded it up, and put it into his pocket-book, from which he took out another paper, and presenting it to the Minister Garat, desired he would deliver that letter immediately to the National Convention. The Minister appearing to hesitate, the King added, 'I will read it you': and without the least change of countenance, read what follows.

'I demand a delay of three days that I may be able to prepare myself for appearing before God. I also for that purpose demand that I may freely see the person whom I shall point out to the Commissioners of the Commune, and that that person may be ensured from all fear and all uneasiness on account of the act of charity he will bestow upon me.

'I demand to be freed from the incessant inspection which the Council General have for some days past established.

'I demand, in that interval, to be empowered to see my Family at the time I shall appoint, and without a witness. I earnestly wish that the National Convention would immediately take into their consideration the state of my Family, and that they may be permitted freely to go wherever they think proper.

'I recommend to the bounty of the Nation at large those persons who were dependent upon me: there are very many of them who had sunk their whole fortune in their places, from the loss of which they must now be in great want; and others who never had anything to live upon but their appointments: among the pensioners, there are many old men, women and children, who have also no other support.

'Done at the Tower of the Temple, the twentieth of January, 1793.   LOUIS.'

Garat took the King's letter, and said he was going with it to the Convention. As he was leaving the room, His Majesty felt again in his pocket, took out his pocket-book, and, presenting a paper from it, said:

'Sir, if the Convention agrees to my demand for the person I desire, here is his address.' He then gave it to a Municipal Officer. This address, written in a different hand from the King's, was: *Monsieur Edgeworth de Firmont, No. 483, Rue du Bacq.* The King went back a few steps, and the Minister, with those who accompanied him, went away.

His Majesty walked about his chamber for an instant. I remained standing against the door, my arms crossed, and as one deprived of all feeling. The King came up to me, and bade me order his dinner. Shortly after, two Municipal Officers called me into the dining-room, where they read me a resolution, importing, 'that Louis should use neither knife nor fork at his meals, but that his valet de chambre should be trusted with a knife to cut his bread and meat, in the presence of two Municipal Officers, and that afterwards the knife should be taken away.' The two Municipal Officers charged me to inform the King of this, which I refused to do.

On entering the dining-room, the King saw the tray on which was the Queen's dinner: he asked why his Family had been made to wait an hour beyond their time, and said the delay would alarm them. He then sat down to table. 'I have no knife', said he. The Municipal Officer, Minier, then mentioned the resolution of the Commune. 'Do they think me such a coward', said the King, 'as to make an attempt on my own life? They have imputed crimes to me, but I am innocent of them, and shall die without fear. Would to God my death might be productive of happiness to the

French, or could avert the miseries I foresee.' A profound silence ensued. The King ate a little: he helped himself to some stewed beef with a spoon, and broke his bread. He was at dinner but a few minutes.

I WAS sitting in my chamber, a prey to the deepest affliction, when about six in the evening, Garat returned to the Tower. I went to announce him to the King, but Santerre, who was before him, walked up to His Majesty, and in a low voice, with a smile upon his face, said: 'Here is the Executive Council.' The Minister, coming forward, told the King that he had carried his letter to the Convention, which had charged him to deliver the following answer: 'That Louis should be at liberty to send for any Minister of religion he should think proper, and to see his Family freely and without witnesses; and that the Nation, ever great and ever just, would take into consideration the state of his Family; that proper indemnification would be granted to the creditors of his household; and that respecting the delay of three days, the National Convention had passed to the order of the day.'

To this reply the King made no observation, but returned to his chamber, where he said to me: 'I thought, from Santerre's air and manner, that he came to inform me of the delay being granted.' A young Municipal Officer, whose name was Botson, seeing the King speak to me, approached us, and the King said to him: 'You seem concerned at my fate; accept my thanks for it.' The Municipal Officer, surprised, knew not what to answer, and I was myself astonished at His Majesty's expressions, for this Municipal Officer, who was scarcely two-and-twenty, and of a mild and engaging figure, had said only a few minutes before: 'I volunteered for duty at the Temple to see the grimaces he will make to-morrow.' It was of the King that he spoke. 'And I too,' added Merceraut, the stone-cutter, whom I mentioned before: 'everybody refused to take the duty; I would not give up this day for a good deal of money.' Such were the vile and ferocious men whom the Commune purposely named to guard the King in his last moments.

For the last four days the King had not seen his Counsel. Such of the Commissioners as had shown themselves concerned for his misfortunes, avoided coming near the place. Among so many subjects to whom he had been a father, among so many Frenchmen whom he had loaded with his bounties, there was but a single servant left with him to participate in his sorrows.

After the answer from the Convention was read, the Commissioners took the Minister of Justice aside, and asked him how the King was to see his Family. 'In private,' replied Garat, 'it is so intended by the Convention.' Upon which the Municipal Officers communicated to him the resolution of the Commune, which enjoined them not to lose sight of the King, night or day. It was then agreed between the Municipal Officers and the Ministers, in order to reconcile these two opposite resolutions, that the King should receive his Family in the dining-room, so as to be seen through the glazed partition, but that the door should be shut that they might not be heard.

His Majesty called the Minister of Justice back, to ask if he had sent to M. de Firmont. Garat said he had brought him with him in his carriage, that he was with the Council, and was coming up. His Majesty gave 3000 livres in gold to a Municipal Officer, named Baudrais, who was talking with the Minister, which he begged him to deliver to M. de Malesherbes, to whom they belonged. The Municipal Officer promised he would, but immediately carried them to the Council, and this money never was paid to M. de Malesherbes. M. de Firmont now made his appearance; the King took him to the turret and shut himself in with him. Garat being gone, there remained in His Majesty's apartment only three Municipal Officers.

At eight o'clock, the King came out of his closet, and desired the Municipal Officers to conduct him to his Family: they replied, that could not be, but his Family should be brought down, if he desired it. 'Be it so,' said the King, 'but I may at least see them alone in my chamber.' 'No,' rejoined one of them, 'we have settled with the Minister of Justice that it shall be in the dining-room.' 'You have heard', said His Majesty, 'that the decree of the Convention permits me to see them without witnesses.' 'True,' replied the Officers, 'you will be in private: the door shall be shut, but we shall have our eyes upon you through the glass.' 'Let my Family come', said the King.

In the interval, His Majesty went into the dining-room: I followed him, placed the table aside, and set

chairs at the top to make room. The King desired me
to bring some water and a glass. There being a carafe
of iced water standing on a table, I brought only a glass,
which I placed by it; on which he told me to bring
water that was not iced, for if the Queen drank that, it
might make her ill. 'Go', added His Majesty, 'and tell
M. de Firmont not to leave the closet, lest my Family
should be shocked on seeing him.' The Commissioner
who had gone for them stayed a quarter of an hour;
during this interval, the King returned to his closet,
but from time to time came to the door in extreme
agitation.

At half-past eight, the door opened. The Queen
came first, leading her son by the hand; Madame
Royale and Madame Elizabeth followed. They all
threw themselves into the arms of the King. A melancholy silence prevailed for some minutes, only broken
by sighs and sobs. The Queen made an inclination
towards His Majesty's chamber. 'No,' said the King,
'let us go into this room, I can see you only there.'
They went in, and I shut the glass door. The King sat
down; the Queen was on his left hand, Madame
Elizabeth on his right, Madame Royale nearly opposite,
and the young Prince stood between his legs. All were
leaning on the King, and often pressed him in their
embraces. This scene of sorrow lasted an hour and
three-quarters, during which it was impossible to hear
anything. It could, however, be seen that after every
sentence uttered by the King, the agitation of the
Queen and Princesses increased, lasted some minutes,
and then the King began to speak again. It was plain,

from their gestures, that they received from himself the first intelligence of his condemnation.

At a quarter past ten, the King rose first; they all followed. I opened the door. The Queen held the King by his right arm: their Majesties gave each a hand to the Dauphin. Madame Royale, on the King's left, had her arms round his body and, behind her, Madame Elizabeth, on the same side, had taken his arm. They advanced some steps towards the door, breaking out into the most agonizing lamentations. 'I assure you', said the King, 'that I will see you again to-morrow morning, at eight o'clock.' 'You promise?' said they all together. 'Yes, I promise.' 'Why not at seven o'clock?' said the Queen. 'Well! yes, at seven,' replied the King, 'farewell!' He pronounced 'farewell' in so impressive a manner that their sobs were renewed, and Madame Royale fainted at the feet of the King, to whom she had clung. I raised her, and assisted Madame Elizabeth to support her. The King, wishing to put an end to this agonizing scene, once more embraced them all most tenderly, and had the resolution to tear himself from their arms. 'Farewell! farewell!' said he, and went into his room.

The Queen, Princesses, and Dauphin, returned to their own apartments. I attempted to continue supporting Madame Royale, but the Municipal Officers stopped me before I had gone up two steps, and compelled me to go in. Though both the doors were shut, the cries and lamentations of the Queen and Princesses were heard for some time on the stairs. The King returned to his Confessor in the turret closet.

He came out in half an hour, and I put supper upon the table: the King ate little, but heartily.

After supper, His Majesty returning to the closet, his Confessor came out in a few minutes, and desired the Municipal Officers to conduct him to the Council Chamber. It was to request that he might be furnished with the garments and whatever else was necessary for performing Mass early the next morning. M. de Firmont did not prevail without great difficulty in having his request granted. The articles wanted for the service were brought from the church of the Capuchins of the Marais, near the Hotel de Soubise, which had been turned into a parish church. On returning from the Council Chamber, M. de Firmont went directly to the King, who accompanied him to the turret, where they remained together till half-past twelve. I then undressed the King, and, as I was going to roll his hair, he said: 'It is not worth the trouble.' Afterwards, when he was in bed, as I was drawing his curtains: 'Cléry, you will call me at five o'clock.'

He was scarcely in bed before he fell into a profound sleep, which lasted, without interruption, till five. M. de Firmont, whom His Majesty had persuaded to take some rest, threw himself upon my bed, and I passed the night on a chair in the King's room, praying God to support his strength and his courage.

The Abbé Edgeworth de Firmont

O N hearing five o'clock strike I began to light the fire. The noise I made awoke the King, who, drawing his curtains, asked if it had struck five. I said it had by several clocks, but not yet by that in the apartment. Having finished with the fire, I went to his bed-side. 'I have slept soundly,' said his Majesty; 'I stood in need of it; yesterday was a fatiguing day to me. Where is M. de Firmont?' I answered, on my bed. 'And where were you all night?' 'On this chair.' 'I am sorry for it', said the King. 'Oh! Sire,' replied I, 'can I think of myself at this moment?' He gave me his hand, and tenderly pressed mine.

I then dressed His Majesty; during which time he took a seal from his watch and put it into his waistcoat pocket; the watch he placed on the chimney-piece: then taking off his ring from his finger, after looking at it again and again, he put it into the pocket with the seal. He changed his shirt, put on a white waistcoat, which he wore the evening before, and I helped him on with his coat. He then emptied his pockets of his pocket-book, his glass, his snuff-box, and some other things, which, with his purse also, he deposited on the chimney-piece: this was all done without a word, and before several Municipal Officers. As soon as he was dressed, the King bade me go and tell M. de Firmont, whom I found already risen, and he immediately attended His Majesty to the turret.

Meanwhile, I placed a chest of drawers in the middle of the chamber, and arranged it in the form of an altar for saying Mass. The necessary articles had been brought at two o'clock in the morning. The Priest's vestments I carried into my chamber, and, when everything was ready, I went and informed His Majesty. He asked me if I was acquainted with the service. I told him I was, but that I did not know the responses by heart. He had a book in his hand, which he opened, and, finding the place of the Mass, gave it me: he then took another book for himself. The Priest was then vesting. Before the altar, I had placed an arm-chair for His Majesty, with a large cushion on the ground: the cushion he desired me to take away, and went himself to his closet for a smaller one, made of hair, which he commonly made use of at his prayers. When the Priest came in, the Municipal Officers retired into the antechamber, and I shut one fold of the door. The Mass began at six o'clock. There was a profound silence during the awful ceremony. The King, all the time on his knees, heard Mass with the most devout attention; and received the Communion. After the service His Majesty withdrew to his closet, and the Priest went into my chamber, to put off his vestments.

I seized this moment for going to the King. He took both my hands into his, and said, with a tone of tenderness, 'Cléry, I am satisfied with your attentions.' 'Ah! Sire,' said I, throwing myself at his feet, 'why cannot I, by my death, satisfy these butchers, and preserve a life of so much value to every good Frenchman? Hope, Sire! they will not dare to strike the blow.' 'Death', said he, 'does not alarm me; I am quite prepared for it; but do not you expose yourself. I mean to request that you should remain with my Son. Take every care of him in this horrid place: bring to his mind, tell him all the pangs I suffered for the misfortunes entailed upon him. The day perhaps may come when he will have it in his power to reward your zeal.' 'Oh! my Master! Oh! my King!' cried I, 'if the most absolute devotion, if my zeal, if my attentions have been agreeable to you, the only reward I desire of your Majesty is to receive your blessing: do not refuse it to the last Frenchman remaining with you.' I was still at his feet, holding one of his hands: in that state he granted my request, and blessed me; then raising me, pressed me to his bosom, saying, 'give it to all who are in my service: and tell Turgy I am pleased with his conduct. Now go,' added he, 'and give no room for suspicion against you.' Then calling me back, and taking up a paper which he had put upon a table: 'Here', said he, 'is a letter I received from Pétion, on your coming to the Temple; it may be of use to you in staying here.' I again seized his hand, which I kissed, and retired. 'Farewell!' he again said to me, 'farewell!'

I went to my room, where I found M. de Firmont on his knees, praying by my bed-side. 'What a Prince!' said he, rising; 'with what resignation and fortitude does he go to meet death! He is as calm, as composed, as if he had been hearing Mass in his own Palace, and surrounded by his Court.' 'I have this moment', said I, 'been taking the most affecting leave of him: he deigned to promise me that he would request my being permitted to continue at the Tower, in the service of his son. I beg you, Sir, when he goes out, to put him in mind of it, for I shall never more have the happiness of seeing him alone.' 'Be composed', said M. de Firmont, and rejoined the King.

At seven o'clock, the King, coming out of his closet, called to me, and taking me within the recess of the window, said: 'You will give this Seal to my Son... this Ring to the Queen, and assure her that it is with pain I part with it...this little packet contains the hair of all my Family, you will give her that too. Tell the Queen, my dear Children, and my Sister, that although I promised to see them this morning I have resolved to spare them the pangs of so cruel a separation: tell them how much it costs me to go without receiving their embraces once more!' He wiped away some tears; then added, in the most mournful accent: 'I charge you to bear them my last farewell!' He returned to the turret.

The Municipal Officers, who had come up, heard His Majesty, and saw him give me the things, which I still held in my hands. At first they desired to have them given up; but one of them proposing to let them remain in my possession till the Council should decide what was to be done, it was so agreed.

In a quarter of an hour the King again came out: 'Enquire', said he to me, 'if I can have a pair of scissors.' I made the request known to the Commissioners. 'Do you know what he wants to do?' 'I know nothing about it.' 'We must know.' I knocked at the door of the closet, and the King came out. The Municipal Officer, who had followed me, said to him: 'You have desired to have a pair of scissors; but, before the request is made to the Council, we must know what you want to do with them.' His Majesty answered: 'It is that Cléry may cut my hair.' The Municipal Officers retired; one of them went down to the Council Chamber, where, after half an hour's deliberation, the scissors were refused. The Officer came up, and acquainted the King with the decision. 'I did not mean to touch the scissors,' said His Majesty; 'I should have desired Cléry to cut my hair before you: try once more, Sir; I beg you to represent my request.' The Officer went back to the Council, who persisted in their refusal.

It was at this time that I was told to prepare myself to accompany the King, in order to undress him on the scaffold. At this intelligence I was seized with terror; but collecting all my strength, I was getting myself ready to discharge this last duty to my Master, who felt a repugnance to its being performed by the executioner, when another Municipal Officer came and told me that I was not to go out, adding: 'The common executioner is good enough for him.'

All the troops in Paris had been under arms from five o'clock in the morning. The beat of drums, the clash of arms, the trampling of horses, the rumbling of cannon, which were incessantly carried from one place to another, all resounded through the Tower.

At half after eight o'clock, the noise increased, the doors were thrown open with great clatter, when Santerre, accompanied by seven or eight Municipal Officers, entered at the head of ten soldiers, and drew them up in two lines. At this movement, the King came out of his closet, and said to Santerre: 'You are come for me?' 'Yes', was the answer. 'A moment', said the King, and went to his closet, from which he instantly returned, followed by his Confessor. His Majesty had his Will in his hand, and addressing a Municipal Officer (named Jacques Roux,* a renegade priest), who happened to stand before the others, said: 'I beg you to give this paper to the Queen—to my wife.' 'It is no business of mine,' replied he, refusing to take it; 'I am come here to conduct you to the scaffold.' His Majesty then turned to Gobeau, another Municipal Officer. 'I beg', said he, 'that you will give this paper to my wife; you may read it; there are some particulars in it I wish to be made known to the Commune.'

I was standing behind the King, near the fireplace, he turned round to me, and I offered him his great-coat. 'I don't want it,' said he, 'give me only my hat.' I presented it to him—his hand met mine, which he pressed once more for the last time. 'Gentlemen,' said he, addressing the Municipal Officers, 'I should be glad that Cléry might stay with my son, as he has been accustomed to be attended by him; I trust that the Commune will grant this request.' His Majesty then looked at Santerre, and said: 'Lead on.'

These were the last words he spoke in his apart-

* Jacques Roux was a member of the Paris commune. During the food shortage of the spring of 1793 Jacques Roux led the extremists or *enragés* in a campaign against monopolists and the high price of bread. As a result, bakers'-shops were sacked, and Roux was evicted from the Commune.

ments. On the top of the stairs he met Mathey, the Warden of the Tower, to whom he said: 'I spoke with some little quickness to you the day before yesterday, do not take it ill.' Mathey made no answer, and even affected to turn from the King while he was speaking.

I remained alone in the chamber, overwhelmed with sorrow, and almost without sense of feeling. The drums and trumpets proclaimed His Majesty's departure from the Tower....An hour after, discharges of artillery, and cries of *Vive la Nation! Vive la République!* were heard....The best of Kings was no more!

THE LAST HOURS OF
LOUIS XVI, KING OF FRANCE

BY
THE ABBÉ EDGEWORTH
DE FIRMONT, HIS CONFESSOR

THE King's fate was not yet decided, when M. de Malesherbes, whom I had not the honour of knowing personally, being able neither to receive me at his house nor to come to mine, arranged a meeting at Madame de Sénozan's. At this meeting M. de Malesherbes gave me a message from the King, in which this unfortunate monarch asked me to attend him on the scaffold. This message was couched in such flattering terms that I would have thought it my duty to suppress it, had it not shown the character of the Prince whose last moments I am about to describe— a Prince who condescended to call this service 'a kindness', and who claimed it as 'a last proof of my attachment to his person; he hoped that I would not refuse; it was only if I felt myself lacking in the necessary courage that he would allow me to find another priest to take my place, and that he would leave me entirely free if I felt I could not undertake the sad duty.'

Such a message would have seemed a most urgent request to anyone; I looked upon it as a command; and I requested M. de Malesherbes to inform His Majesty, if he had means to do so, that I should do everything that a heart broken with sadness could dictate in such circumstances.

Several days passed, and hearing nothing further, I began to hope that the sentence might only be one of deportation, or that at any rate there might be time allowed for reflection, when on January 20, at four o'clock in the afternoon, a man unknown to me called at my house and handed me a note from the

Provisional Executive Council, which read as follows:
'The Executive Council, having business of the greatest
importance to communicate to Citizen Edgeworth de
Firmont, requests him to appear before them immediately.' The messenger added that he had orders
to accompany me, and that a carriage was waiting in
the street. I immediately left with him.

On arriving at the Tuileries, where the Council was
sitting, I found all the Ministers assembled. The
moment I entered the room, they rose and surrounded
me. The Minister of Justice asked me: 'Are you
Citizen Edgeworth de Firmont?' I replied, 'Yes.'
'Louis Capet', he said, 'having expressed a wish
that you should be with him during his last hours, we
have asked you here to know if you are willing to do
him the service he asks?' 'Since the King has expressed this wish, and asked for me by name,' I replied,
'to do so is my duty.'

'In that case,' said the Minister, 'come with me to
the Temple, for I am going there now.'

He lifted up a bundle of papers from his desk,
conferred for a moment or two with the other Ministers
in a low voice, and telling me to follow him, left the
room abruptly.

An escort of cavalry was awaiting us with the
Minister's carriage; I got in, and he followed me. I was
wearing lay dress, as were all the Catholic clergy of
Paris at that time; but thinking on the one hand of
what I owed to a King who was not accustomed to
seeing priests so dressed, and on the other of religion
itself, which was receiving for the first time a sort of

recognition from the new Government, I thought I had the right to assume, for this occasion at any rate, the outward signs of my Orders, or at least to make an attempt to do so: I looked upon it as my duty. I spoke to this effect to the Minister before we left the Tuileries, but he refused me permission in words which gave me no opportunity of insisting, but without any offensive remarks.

The journey passed for the most part in silence; though two or three times the Minister tried to break it. 'Heavens!' he said, after carefully shutting the carriage windows, 'what a fearful task I have!... What a man!' he added, speaking of the King, 'what resignation, what bravery! No, Nature alone could not give him such courage: there must be something superhuman in it.' Such remarks gave me a perfect opportunity of entering into conversation with him, and of telling him painful truths. But I hesitated for a moment before speaking; then, remembering that my duty lay in procuring for the King the consolations of religion for which he had asked so devoutly, and that any remarks of mine might have the result of preventing me from fulfilling this duty, I kept silence. The Minister seemed to understand what my silence meant, and did not speak again on the journey.

We arrived at the Temple without another word spoken. The outer door was at once opened to us, but as soon as we arrived at the building which divides the courtyard from the garden we were stopped. Here was the enquiry office, and to pass beyond it visitors had to state their business and be recognised by the Commissioners. The Minister himself was subjected to this enquiry, just as I was. We had to wait for the officials for almost a quarter of an hour, and still never a word passed between us. At last they came. There were two of them; one was a youth of seventeen or eighteen. They greeted the Minister, whom they recognised; he in his turn introduced me, and said who I was and why I was there. The officials signed to me to follow them, and all together we crossed the garden and entered the courtyard.

The door of the tower, although extremely small and very low, was so heavily weighted with iron bars and bolts that it opened with an excruciating noise. We crossed a hall filled with guards, and entered a second and larger one, which from its shape looked to me as if it had once been a chapel. Here the officials of the Commune, who were responsible for the King, were gathered together. Although much nearer to them, I could not see in any of them the disquiet and embarrassment which I had noticed in the Ministers at the Tuileries. There were about twelve of them, for the most part wearing Jacobin costume. Their air, their manners, their *sang-froid*—all showed them to be of a type which the greatest of crimes would not appal. In all fairness, however, I must admit that this did not appear to apply to them all, for I saw some amongst them whom weakness alone seemed to have brought to this place of horror.

Be that as it may, the Minister took them all with him into a corner of the room, and there read to them, in a low voice, the papers he had brought with him from the Tuileries, after which he turned to me and told me abruptly to follow him. To this the officials objected, and they again gathered in the corner and whispered amongst themselves, after which half of them accompanied the Minister, and the other half stayed behind to guard me.

As soon as the Minister had left the room, and the doors were securely shut, the oldest of the officials came up to me, and with an air of embarrassment spoke to me of the terrible responsibility which I was undertaking, excused himself for the liberty he had been forced to take, etc. I understood that this meant that they were going to search me, and I forestalled him by saying to him that M. de Malesherbes's reputation not having been sufficient to exempt him from this formality, I should not be flattered if they made an exception of me; I added that I had nothing in my pockets that they could possibly suspect, as they could very easily ascertain. Despite this, however, a very rigorous search was made. My tobacco box was opened, and the tobacco sifted. A little pencil in a steel case, which happened to be in my pocket, was subjected to the most careful examination, for fear that it might have contained a dagger. But my papers did not interest my searchers in the least. As soon as the search was over, they again apologised for having troubled me, and offered me a chair, but no sooner was I seated than two of the officials who had gone into the King's apartments came down again to tell me that I now had permission to see him.

They conducted me upstairs by a circular staircase so narrow that two persons could hardly pass on it. Every now and then the staircase was barred, and at each of these barriers stood a sentry. These men were real *sans-culottes*, nearly all drunk, and their shouts, echoed by the stone roof, were quite terrifying. On arriving at His Majesty's rooms, the doors of which were all open, I saw the King in the middle of a group of eight or ten persons. This group consisted of the Minister of Justice (Garat the younger), and several members of the Commune, who had come to read to the King the fatal decree fixing his execution for the next day.

His Majesty was standing in the middle of them, calm, quiet, even gracious; not one of the officials looked calmer than he. When I entered, he signed with his hand to them to leave him; they obeyed in silence; he closed the door after them, and I was alone with him.

Till then I had been occupied solely with my own feelings, but at the sight of this Prince, formerly so great and now so wretched, I could no longer hold back my tears: they streamed down my face and I fell at his feet, unable to express myself save in the language of grief. The sight of my emotion affected him far more deeply than the decree which had just been read to him. At first he only answered my tears with his own, but soon, recovering himself, he said, 'Forgive this weakness, if it can be so called; for a long while I have lived surrounded by my enemies, and custom has to some extent familiarised me with them; but the sight of a loyal subject is too much for me: it is a

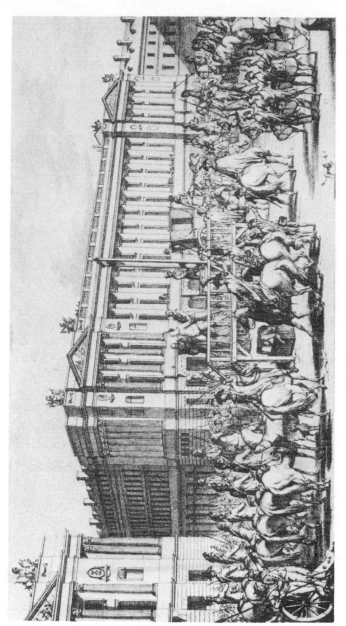

The King on the Scaffold

sight to which I am no longer accustomed and touches me deeply despite myself.'

Saying this, he raised me with much kindness, and led me into his cabinet, for in his room everything could be overheard. This cabinet was contrived in one of the turrets of the Temple; it had neither curtains nor ornaments: an inefficient porcelain stove took the place of a fire, and the only furniture were a table and three chairs covered with leather. He made me sit down near him: 'You can understand, Monsieur,' he said, 'that there is only one thing which occupies me now, the only important thing that remains, for what is everything else beside this? But I must ask you to wait for a few minutes, for my family are just coming. While you wait, please look at this paper; I am happy to be able to show it to you.' His Majesty took from his pocket a folded paper, broke the seal, and handed it to me.

It was his Will, which he had made the previous December, at a time when he did not think he would be allowed the services of a Catholic priest to attend him in his last moments—his last struggle. Everyone who has read this document, so worthy of a Christian monarch, will be able to imagine the deep impression which it made on me; but what will amaze them is to learn that the King had the courage himself to read it to me, not once but twice. His voice did not falter and his expression never changed, except when he read the names of those most dear to him. Then he could not go on, and his tears flowed in spite of himself; but when he referred only to himself and his own sufferings he did not seem any more affected than a man ordinarily would be on hearing of the miseries of another.

When he had finished reading, since his family had not yet arrived, he asked me for news as to the position of the clergy and the situation of the Church in France. Despite the closeness of his confinement, he had managed to get some news of it; he had learnt that the French ecclesiastics, obliged to flee, had received a welcome in London, but he was quite ignorant of the details. What I was able to tell him made a deep impression upon him, and while deploring the fate of the French clergy, he did not fail to pay tribute to the generosity of the English people who had endeavoured to soften their hard lot. But he was not satisfied with general questions, and coming to points of greater detail in a way that astonished me, he asked me what had happened to certain clergy in whom he took a more personal interest. He asked after Cardinal de la Rochefoucauld and the Bishop of Clermont; and particularly after the Archbishop of Paris.

The King asked me where he was, what he was doing, and whether I had any means of corresponding with him. 'Impress on him', he said, 'that I die in the Faith, and that I have never recognised any other pastor than he. He will remember that I never answered his last letter; I was still at the Tuileries at the time; and, indeed, events were pressing me so hard just then that I could not find the time. He will forgive me, I'm sure; he is so kind.' The Abbé de F... was also referred to. The King had never seen him, but he was aware of all the services that this priest had rendered to the diocese of Paris in these difficult times. He asked me what had become of him, and when I said that he had had the good fortune to escape, he spoke of him in terms that showed the importance he attached to his safety and the regard he had for his great qualities.

The conversation then changed to the subject of the Duke of Orléans. 'What have I ever done to my cousin', said the King to me, 'that he should seek my downfall?...But after all, he is more to be pitied than I. My position is tragic, no doubt, but most certainly I would not change it for his.'

This most interesting conversation was interrupted by one of the officials, who came to tell the King that his family had now come down, and that he had permission to see them. Very affected, he left instantly. The interview took place (as far as I could gather, for I was not present myself) in a little room only separated by a glass screen from that occupied by the Commissioners, in order that they might be able to see and hear what was going on. I myself, although in the cabinet in which the King left me, easily distinguished the voices, and in spite of myself was a witness to the most touching scene which I ever experienced. No pen could describe it; for more than half an hour not a single distinguishable word was said; nor were there tears or sobs; but loud cries—loud enough to be heard outside the Tower. The King, the Queen, Madame Elizabeth, the Dauphin and Madame Royale—all lamented together. At last their cries and tears stopped for lack of strength, and they began to talk, quietly, their voices low and controlled.

Their talk lasted about an hour, after which the King said good-bye, letting them think they would see him again the next day. After they had left, he came back at once to me, in a state of agitation that showed how unendurable the parting had been to him. 'Ah, Monsieur,' he said to me, throwing himself into a chair, 'what an interview I have just had! Why should I love and be so tenderly loved? But now let us forget all save the fact of salvation; that now needs all my thoughts and desires.'

He went on speaking to me in this strain, in terms which showed his feelings and his courage, when Cléry came in to suggest that he should take supper. The King hesitated for a moment, and then agreed. Supper did not take more than five minutes, and then on returning to the cabinet, he suggested I should have something as well. Although I had no appetite, I thought I ought to obey his wish, or at least make a semblance of so doing.

One particular thought had been for a long time in the forefront of my mind, especially since I had actually been in the King's presence; it was to procure for him the Holy Communion, of which he had been so long deprived, no matter at what cost to myself. I would have been able to bring the Host with me secretly, as one had to do in the case of many persons who were under house-arrest; but the strict search which one had to undergo on entering the Temple, and the sacrilege which would have been the inevitable result, had prevented me from doing so. Consequently there was nothing else to do but to say Mass in the King's room, if I could find the means.

I suggested this to him, but at first he seemed reluctant at the idea; however, since he so earnestly desired it, and I realised that his opposition only came from the fear of compromising me, I begged him to give me *carte blanche*, promising that I would use all discretion and prudence. He replied, 'Very well, Monsieur, but I am afraid you will not succeed, for I know the men to whom you will have to apply, and they will never give permission for anything that they have the power to refuse.'

Having received the King's permission, I asked to be taken to the Council Chamber, where I made the request in his name. Since the Commissioners of the Tower were not in the least prepared for it, my demand disconcerted them greatly; they searched for various pretexts to avoid agreeing. 'Where could a Priest be found as late as this?' they asked me. 'And when he is found, where could one find the necessary ornaments?' 'The Priest is found,' I replied, 'since I am here; as for the ornaments, the nearest Church will supply them; there is nothing to do but to send for them: for the rest, my request is reasonable, and it would be against your own principles to refuse it.'

One of the Commissioners, in most carefully chosen words, gave me to understand that he considered my request to be nothing but a trap, and that under the pretext of giving Communion to the King, I intended to poison him. 'History', he said, 'gives us enough examples of such a thing to make us extremely hesitant.' Looking at him, I said, 'The strict search which I underwent when I came in will surely prove to you that

I have no poison on me; if then any is found to-morrow, it will be from you that I shall have received it, since everything I ask for will necessarily pass through your hands.' He began to reply, but the others stopped him, and as a last excuse told me that the members of the Council not being all present, they could not at the moment give me a definite answer, but that they would ask the absent members to attend, and would then let me know their decision.

After a quarter of an hour I was again brought in, and the President said, 'Citizen Minister of Religion, the Council has considered the request you have made in the name of Louis Capet, and has decided that since the request is in conformity with the laws giving freedom of religion, it will be granted. There are, however, two conditions; first, that you will imme-diately draw up this request in writing, and sign it; secondly, that the religious service will be finished not later than seven o'clock to-morrow morning, because at eight o'clock exactly Louis Capet will leave for the place of execution.' These last words were spoken with the cold-bloodedness characteristic of a mind which could regard the greatest crimes without a trace of remorse. I wrote my request and signed it, and put it on the desk.

They at once brought me back to the King who was awaiting the result with considerable anxiety. The brief account which I gave him, leaving out any men-tion of the conditions, seemed to afford him the greatest happiness.

It was then a little after ten o'clock. I stayed with

His Majesty until well into the night, when seeing him tired, I suggested to him that he should take a little rest. He agreed, and told me to do the same.

At his orders I went into the little room that Cléry occupied; it was only separated from the King's room by a partition; and while I was a prey to the most tormenting thoughts, I heard the King quietly giving his orders for the next morning, go to bed, and fall into a peaceful and deep sleep.

At five o'clock His Majesty rose and dressed. Shortly afterwards he sent for me, and kept me nearly an hour in the cabinet in which he had received me the previous evening. On leaving this room, I found an altar erected in the King's bedroom. The Commissioners had sent everything I had requested; they had even done rather more, for I had only asked for the merest necessities.

The King heard Mass kneeling on the floor, without a *prie-Dieu* or even a cushion; he made his Communion; after which I left him alone for a short time while he finished his devotions. Soon he sent for me again, and I found him seated beside the stove, trying to get warm. 'How happy I am', he said to me, 'that I have been able to act in accordance with my principles! Without them, where should I be at this moment? But now, how sweet death seems to me, for there exists on high an incorruptible judge who will give me the justice that has been refused to me on earth.'

My ministry to my King only allows me to quote certain scattered remarks of different conversations

which he had with me during the sixteen last hours of
his life;* but one can judge of what I could add, if
I were permitted to tell all he said.

Dawn began to break, and the General Assembly
sounded in every part of Paris. It was heard very
distinctly in the Tower, and I can assure my readers
that my blood froze in my veins: the King, much
calmer than I, after listening for a moment, said to me
without any apparent emotion, 'It is probably the
National Guard assembling.' Soon after, detachments
of cavalry entered the courtyard, and one could distinctly hear the voices of the officers and the movement
of the horses. The King listened again, and said with
the same calm, 'I think they are approaching.'

When he saw her the previous night, he had promised the Queen that he would see her again in the
morning, and was anxious to keep his word, but I most
urgently begged him not to give her this additional
agony, which would be almost unbearable for her. He
remained silent a moment, and then, with an expression
of the deepest sadness, said, 'You are right; it would be
unendurable for her. It would be better to deprive
myself of the happiness of seeing her once again, and
to let her live in hope a little longer.'

Between seven o'clock and eight several persons
came and knocked on the door, under different pretexts; each time I feared it was the last; but the King,
much calmer than I, went himself to the door and
answered their inquiries. I do not know who the
persons were, but amongst them were undoubtedly

* The Abbé de Firmont refers to the seal of the confessional.

some of the most revolting monsters fathered by the Revolution, for I heard one of them say, in a mocking tone—*à propos* of what I do not know—'Oh, oh, that was all very fine when you were a King; but you aren't one any more!' His Majesty did not reply, but on returning to me he shrugged his shoulders and said, 'You see how these people treat me; but one must know how to suffer all insults.'

Another time, after having answered one of the Commissioners who came and interrupted him, he said to me, smiling, 'These people see daggers and poison everywhere; they are afraid I am going to kill myself. They don't know me; to kill myself would be an act of weakness: since I have to, I shall know how to die.'

The final knock on the door was Santerre and his men. The King opened the door, and they said (but I do not know what words they used) that it was time to go. 'I am occupied for a moment,' he said to them in an authoritative tone, 'wait for me here; I shall be with you in a minute.' He shut the door, and coming to me, knelt in front of me. 'It is finished,' he said;* 'give me your last blessing, and pray to God that He will uphold me to the end.'

In a moment or two he rose, and leaving the cabinet walked towards the group of men who were in the bedroom. Their faces showed the most complete assurance; and they all remained covered. Seeing this, the King asked for his hat. While Cléry, with tears running down his face, hurried to look for it, 'If one

---

* The King used the last words of Our Lord on the Cross; in French, *Tout est consommé.*

of you', said the King, 'is a member of the Commune, I ask you to take charge of this paper.'

It was his Will, which one of them took from the King's hand.* 'I also recommend to the Commune my valet, Cléry, for whose services to me I can never be sufficiently grateful. Please be kind enough to give him my watch and all my effects, both those which are here and those which have been sent to the Commune; I should also be grateful if in recompense for all his services to me he might be allowed to enter the service of the Queen—of my wife.' (The King used both words.) Nobody replied. After a moment, in a firm tone the King said, 'Let us go.'

At these words, everybody went out. The King crossed the first courtyard (formerly the garden) on foot; he turned once or twice towards the Tower, as if to say a last good-bye to all that he held dear in this world; his every movement showed that he was calling up all his reserves of strength and courage.

At the entrance of the second courtyard was a coach; two gendarmes were standing beside its door. When the King approached, one of them got in and sat down on the little seat with his back to the horses; the King then took his place opposite, placing me beside him, and the other gendarme sat down beside his comrade, and shut the door. It is said that one of these gendarmes

---

* Jacques Roux, in the account he gave to the Commune the same day, boasted of having answered, 'We are not here to take your orders, but to bring you to the scaffold.' I did not myself hear the words, but one who could dare to boast of such an answer could easily have said it. (*Note by de Firmont.*)

was a Priest disguised: I can only hope, for the honour of the priesthood, that the story is untrue. It is also said that they had orders to kill the King if they observed the least movement amongst the onlookers. I do not know if this was true, but it seems to me that unless they had other arms on them than those which were visible, it would have been exceedingly difficult to carry out such a design, for they seemed to have only muskets, which it would have been impossible to use.

The movement that was feared was not altogether imaginary; a large number of persons devoted to the King had determined to snatch him by force from the hands of the executioners or at least to dare all with that intent. Two of the leaders, young men of a very well-known name, had come to warn me of this the day before, and without being entirely sanguine, I did not give up all hope until we reached the very foot of the scaffold.

I have since learned that the orders of the Commune, for this terrible morning, had been so carefully conceived and so rigidly executed that of the four or five hundred persons who were sworn to attempt a rescue, only twenty-five were able to reach the rendezvous; all the rest, by reason of the measures taken throughout the city, could not even leave their houses.

The King, finding himself shut in a coach where he could neither speak to me nor hear me without witnesses to our conversation, kept silence. I handed him my breviary, the only book I had with me. He gratefully accepted it; he seemed to wish me to point out the psalms which were best suited to the situation, and recited them alternately with me. The gendarmes, also remaining silent, seemed amazed at the calmness and piety of a monarch whom they had no doubt never seen so close at hand before.

The drive lasted nearly two hours. All the streets were lined with citizens, armed, some with pikes and some with muskets. The coach itself was surrounded by a large body of troops, no doubt drawn from the most corrupt and revolutionary in Paris. As an additional precaution, a number of drummers marched in front of the horses, in order to prevent any shouts being heard that might be raised in the King's favour. But there were no shouts; not a soul was to be seen in the doorways or in the windows; no one was in the streets save those armed citizens who, no doubt through fear and weakness, connived at a crime which perhaps many of them detested in their hearts.

The coach arrived, amid a great silence, at the *Place Louis XV*,* and stopped in the middle of a wide empty space which had been left round the scaffold; this space was edged with cannon; and beyond, as far as the eye could reach, one saw an armed multitude.

As soon as the King felt the coach coming to a stop, he leaned over to me and said in a whisper, 'We have arrived, if I'm not mistaken.' My silence said yes. One of the executioners came forward to open the door of the coach, but the King stopped him, and putting his hand on my knee, said to the gendarmes, 'Messieurs, I commend this gentleman to your care; be good

* Now the Place de la Concorde.

enough to see that after my death he is not offered any insult; I charge you to see to this.' As the gendarmes did not reply, the King began to say it again in a louder voice, but was interrupted by one of them saying, 'Yes, yes, we'll take care of that; leave it to us.' I must add that he said it in a tone of voice which would have frozen me, if at such a moment it had been possible for me to think of myself.

As soon as the King had got out of the coach, three of the executioners surrounded him, and tried to remove his outer clothes. He pushed them away with dignity, and took off his coat himself. He also took off his collar and his shirt, and made himself ready with his own hands. The executioners, disconcerted for a moment by the King's proud bearing, recovered themselves and surrounded him again in order to bind his hands. 'What are you doing?' said the King, quickly drawing his hands back. 'Binding your hands', answered one of them. 'Binding me!' said the King, in a voice of indignation, 'never! Do what you have been ordered, but you shall never bind me.' The executioners insisted; they spoke more loudly, and seemed about to call for help to force the King to obey.

This was the most agonising moment of this terrible morning; one minute more, and the best of Kings would have received an outrage a thousand times worse than death, by the violence that they were going to use towards him. He seemed to fear this himself, and turning his head, seemed to be asking my advice. At first I remained silent, but when he continued to look at me, I said, with tears in my eyes,

'Sire, in this new outrage I see one last resemblance between Your Majesty and the God Who is about to be your reward.'

At these words he raised his eyes to heaven with an expression of unutterable sadness. 'Surely', he replied, 'it needs nothing less than His example to make me submit to such an insult.' Then, turning to the executioners, 'Do what you will; I will drink the cup, even to the dregs.'

The steps of the scaffold were extremely steep. The King was obliged to lean on my arm, and from the difficulty they caused him, I feared that his courage was beginning to wane: but what was my astonishment when, arrived at the top, he let go of me, crossed the scaffold with a firm step, silenced with a glance the fifteen or twenty drummers who had been placed directly opposite, and in a voice so loud that it could be heard as far away as the *Pont-tournant*, pronounced these unforgettable words, 'I die innocent of all the crimes with which I am charged. I forgive those who are guilty of my death, and I pray God that the blood which you are about to shed may never be required of France.'

POSTSCRIPT

AFTER the King's execution, the revolutionaries had to contend not only with most of the rest of Europe, who were horrified by the murder, but also with a number of malcontents in their own country. The 'Mountain', as the extreme party was called, entered into a life and death struggle with the moderates, the 'Girondists', and on the outbreak of the insurrection in the Vendée accused the moderates of being the accomplices of the Vendéens. On 2 June 1793, the Girondists were totally defeated, and the government of France was in the hands of the extremists.

On 2 August the Convention ordered the trial of Marie Antoinette before the Revolutionary Tribunal, and brought her to the prison of the Conciergerie. The story of her trial and the infamous charges brought against her is too well known to need repetition; nine months after the King's death, the Queen was guillotined.

Of the rest of the chief actors in the tragic story, Madame Elizabeth was tried by the Revolutionary Tribunal and put to death on 10 May 1794, and the young Dauphin, in the eyes of the legitimists King Louis XVII, was officially declared to have died in the Temple prison. What really happened to him is unknown. A number of persons claimed to be the son of Louis XVI after the Restoration, and these various claims have led to much controversy. A whole library of books have been written upon this much-vexed question, and a number of law-suits have occurred, but no certain answer has ever been given, and presumably none ever will.

Only Madame Royale, the King's daughter, escaped with her life, being released in December 1795, as an exchange against the French hostages held by the Austrian government.

As for Cléry; after the King's death, Marie Antoinette asked to be allowed to see him in order that she might hear from his lips her husband's last words on the scaffold. But this was refused her. On the evening of the same day, Cléry was forced to sit at supper with Santerre and listen to the Republican general boasting of having drowned the King's last words with a roll of drums. The poor valet de chambre fainted with grief and shock, and one of the few men of decent feeling among the Municipal Officers, Goret, revived him with brandy, and spent the night at his bedside.

Cléry remained in the Temple prison till March 1793, nearly two months after the execution of the King. On his release, he retired to his house at Juvisy, and soon after made a courageous though unsuccessful attempt to gain access to the Queen, who had been transferred to the Conciergerie. In May, he was again arrested and incarcerated in La Force prison. His life was saved by the revolution of Thermidor (August 1794), which ended the Terror.

In the summer of 1795, hearing that Madame Royale was to be freed, Cléry decided to try and join her, and moved to Strasbourg, where his brother was an army contractor. He took with him a trunk, filled with the sad remnants of the captivity in the Temple: rags, and scribbled notes. It was at Strasbourg, from these notes, that Cléry wrote his memoirs. He had just finished these when he learnt that the princess had been handed over, and shortly after he was able to join her outside Vienna. Cléry then carried despatches from the princess to her brother Louis XVIII, who welcomed him and employed him on several secret missions.

In a note to the original edition Cléry recounts the following story. 'Having left Vienna to go to London', he writes, 'I went to Blankenburg for the purpose of laying my manuscript at the King's feet. When his Majesty came to this part of my journal [Louis XVI's request that Cléry should give his seal to the Dauphin and his ring to the Queen], he looked into his desk, and, with emotion, showing me a seal, asked me if I recollected it? I replied, it was the same. "If you could doubt it," continued the King, "read this note." I trembled as I took it. I recognised the Queen's writing; and the note was likewise signed by the Dauphin, at the time he was Louis XVII, by Madame Royale, and by Madame Elizabeth. It may be imagined what I felt! I was in the presence of a Prince whom fate tires not in pursuing. I had just parted with the Abbé de Firmont, and it was on the twenty-first of January that in the hands of Louis XVIII I again met with this ensign of royalty, which Louis XVI had been solicitous to preserve for his son.... I attended the mass which the King caused to be solemnized by the Abbé de Firmont, on the day of his brother's martyrdom. The tears I there saw shed are not foreign to my subject.'

The memoirs were published in London in 1798. They enjoyed tremendous success from the beginning, and were translated into most European languages. As a mark of his appreciation, Louis XVIII made Cléry a Knight of the Order of St Louis. The French government, however, was alarmed at the reaction in the King's favour produced by the publication of the memoirs, and caused a spurious edition to be printed containing a distorted account of the facts.

In 1801 Cléry returned to Paris, where he attempted to publish a new edition of his memoirs, but was refused permission to do so unless he included an apology for the new régime. He was then offered the post of First Chamberlain to the future Empress Josephine, which, however, he refused on account of his fidelity to his legitimate sovereign. It was on account of Napoleon's anger at his refusal that Cléry finally left France. He spent his latter years in Vienna, where he died in 1809.

After the King's execution, De Firmont refused to leave France, and in spite of the danger he ran, he continued a secret correspondence with Princess Elizabeth. But in 1796, after the death of his mother in prison, he escaped to England, bringing with him the Princess's last message to her brother, the future King Charles X, who was then in Edinburgh. He then left for Blankenburg, to be with the *de jure* King, Louis XVIII, with whom he spent ten years. He caught a fever while attending some wounded French prisoners in the town, and died in May 1807, at the age of sixty-two.

The elder branch of his family, of which the novelist, Maria Edgeworth, is the best known, remained true to the Protestant faith, and continued to live in Ireland.

The reader will note that De Firmont himself makes no mention of the famous words of farewell to the King that have been so often attributed to him, 'Son of Saint Louis, ascend to heaven!' These words are not only recorded by royalist sympathizers, D'Allonville, Bertrand de Molleville, Beaulieu, Montjoie and Madame Royale herself, but by revolutionary writers as well, such as Mercier, who quoted the exact phrase in his *Nouveau Paris*. When questioned on the point, De Firmont said on several occasions that he was so overcome with grief and horror at the time that he had no clear knowledge of what he had said; but there is no doubt but that the words ascribed to him were circulated all over Paris immediately after the King's death, and never authoritatively denied. Certainly Sanson, the executioner, speaking many years afterwards to Louis XVIII, assured him that he had himself clearly heard De Firmont using the words quoted.

PRINTED IN ENGLAND